YOU
CAN'T
KEEP
A
GOOD
WOMAN
DOWN

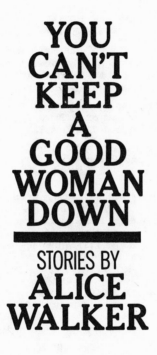

YOU CAN'T KEEP A GOOD WOMAN DOWN

STORIES BY
ALICE WALKER

Harcourt Brace Jovanovich
New York and London

A number of these stories were previously published, in *Ms., Mother Jones, Essence, Conditions,* and *Prisma.* "Coming Apart" was first published as "A Fable."

Library of Congress Cataloging in Publication Data
Walker, Alice, 1944–
You can't keep a good woman down.
CONTENTS: Nineteen fifty-five.—How
did I get away with killing one of
the biggest lawyers in the state?
It was easy.—Elethia.—[etc.]
I. Title.
PS3573.A425Y6   813'.54   80-8761
ISBN 0-15-199754-3

Printed in the United States of America

First edition

B C D E

This book is dedicated to my contemporaries

I thank my sister Ruth for the stories she tells.

I thank Bessie Head, Ama Ata Aidoo, Buchi Emecheta, Wa Thiong'o Ngugi, Okot p'Bitek and Ousmane Sembene for the stories they write.

I thank Gloria Steinem, Joanne Edgar and Suzanne Braun Levine of *Ms.* magazine, who greeted each of the many stories *Ms.* published from this collection with sisterly welcome and enthusiasm.

I thank Ma Rainey, Bessie (*A Good Man Is Hard to Find*) Smith, Mamie Smith and Perry (*You Can't Keep a Good Man Down*) Bradford, among others of their generation, for insisting on the value and beauty of the authentic.

CONTENTS

ix

Contents

*It is harder to kill something
that is spiritually alive
than it is to bring the dead
back to life.*

—*Hermann Hesse*

YOU
CAN'T
KEEP
A
GOOD
WOMAN
DOWN

NINETEEN
FIFTY-FIVE

1955

The car is a brandnew red Thunderbird convertible, and it's passed the house more than once. It slows down real slow now, and stops at the curb. An older gentleman dressed like a Baptist deacon gets out on the side near the house, and a young fellow who looks about sixteen gets out on the driver's side. They are white, and I wonder what in the world they doing in this neighborhood.

Well, I say to J. T., put your shirt on, anyway, and let me clean these glasses offa the table.

We had been watching the ballgame on TV. I wasn't actually watching, I was sort of daydreaming, with my foots up in J. T.'s lap.

I seen 'em coming on up the walk, brisk, like they coming to sell something, and then they rung the bell, and

3

J. T. declined to put on a shirt but instead disappeared into the bedroom where the other television is. I turned down the one in the living room; I figured I'd be rid of these two double quick and J. T. could come back out again.

Are you Gracie Mae Still? asked the old guy, when I opened the door and put my hand on the lock inside the screen.

And I don't need to buy a thing, said I.

What makes you think we're sellin'? he asks, in that hearty Southern way that makes my eyeballs ache.

Well, one way or another and they're inside the house and the first thing the young fellow does is raise the TV a couple of decibels. He's about five feet nine, sort of womanish looking, with real dark white skin and a red pouting mouth. His hair is black and curly and he looks like a Loosianna creole.

About one of your songs, says the deacon. He is maybe sixty, with white hair and beard, white silk shirt, black linen suit, black tie and black shoes. His cold gray eyes look like they're sweating.

One of my songs?

Traynor here just *loves* your songs. Don't you, Traynor? He nudges Traynor with his elbow. Traynor blinks, says something I can't catch in a pitch I don't register.

The boy learned to sing and dance livin' round you people out in the country. Practically cut his teeth on you.

Traynor looks up at me and bites his thumbnail.

I laugh.

Well, one way or another they leave with my agreement that they can record one of my songs. The deacon writes me a check for five hundred dollars, the boy grunts his awareness of the transaction, and I am laughing all over myself by the time I rejoin J. T.

4

Just as I am snuggling down beside him though I hear the front door bell going off again.

Forgit his hat? asks J. T.

I hope not, I say.

The deacon stands there leaning on the door frame and once again I'm thinking of those sweaty-looking eyeballs of his. I wonder if sweat makes your eyeballs pink because his are sure pink. Pink and gray and it strikes me that nobody I'd care to know is behind them.

I forgot one little thing, he says pleasantly. I forgot to tell you Traynor and I would like to buy up all of those records you made of the song. I tell you we sure do love it.

Well, love it or not, I'm not so stupid as to let them do that without making 'em pay. So I says, Well, that's gonna cost you. Because, really, that song never did sell all that good, so I was glad they was going to buy it up. But on the other hand, them two listening to my song by themselves, and nobody else getting to hear me sing it, give me a pause.

Well, one way or another the deacon showed me where I would come out ahead on any deal he had proposed so far. Didn't I give you five hundred dollars? he asked. What white man—and don't even need to mention colored—would give you more? We buy up all your records of that particular song: first, you git royalties. Let me ask you, how much you sell that song for in the first place? Fifty dollars? A hundred, I say. And no royalties from it yet, right? Right. Well, when we buy up all of them records you gonna git royalties. And that's gonna make all them race record shops sit up and take notice of Gracie Mae Still. And they gonna push all them other records of yourn they got. And you no doubt will become one of the big name colored recording artists. And then we can offer you another five hundred dollars for letting us do all this for you. And by God you'll be sittin' pretty! You can go out and buy you the kind of outfit a star should have. Plenty sequins and yards of red satin.

I had done unlocked the screen when I saw I could get some more money out of him. Now I held it wide open while he squeezed through the opening between me and the door. He whipped out another piece of paper and I signed it.

He sort of trotted out to the car and slid in beside Traynor, whose head was back against the seat. They swung around in a u-turn in front of the house and then they was gone.

J. T. was putting his shirt on when I got back to the bedroom. Yankees beat the Orioles 10–6, he said. I believe I'll drive out to Paschal's pond and go fishing. Wanta go?

While I was putting on my pants J. T. was holding the two checks.

I'm real proud of a woman that can make cash money without leavin' home, he said. And I said *Umph*. Because we met on the road with me singing in first one little low-life jook after another, making ten dollars a night for myself if I was lucky, and sometimes bringin' home nothing but my life. And J. T. just loved them times. The way I was fast and flashy and always on the go from one town to another. He loved the way my singin' made the dirt farmers cry like babies and the womens shout Honey, hush! But that's mens. They loves any style to which you can get 'em accustomed.

1956

My little grandbaby called me one night on the phone: Little Mama, Little Mama, there's a white man on the television singing one of your songs! Turn on channel 5.

Lord, if it wasn't Traynor. Still looking half asleep from the neck up, but kind of awake in a nasty way from the waist down. He wasn't doing too bad with my song either,

6

but it wasn't just the song the people in the audience was screeching and screaming over, it was that nasty little jerk he was doing from the waist down.

Well, Lord have mercy, I said, listening to him. If I'da closed my eyes, it could have been me. He had followed every turning of my voice, side streets, avenues, red lights, train crossings and all. It give me a chill.

Everywhere I went I heard Traynor singing my song, and all the little white girls just eating it up. I never had so many ponytails switched across my line of vision in my life. They was so *proud*. He was a *genius*.

Well, all that year I was trying to lose weight anyway and that and high blood pressure and sugar kept me pretty well occupied. Traynor had made a smash from a song of mine, I still had seven hundred dollars of the original one thousand dollars in the bank, and I felt if I could just bring my weight down, life would be sweet.

1957

I lost ten pounds in 1956. That's what I give myself for Christmas. And J. T. and me and the children and their friends and grandkids of all description had just finished dinner—over which I had put on nine and a half of my lost ten—when who should appear at the front door but Traynor. Little Mama, Little Mama! It's that white man who sings ———— ———— ————. The children didn't call it my song anymore. Nobody did. It was funny how that happened. Traynor and the deacon had bought up all my records, true, but on his record he had put "written by Gracie Mae Still." But that was just another name on the label, like "produced by Apex Records."

On the TV he was inclined to dress like the deacon told him. But now he looked presentable.

Merry Christmas, said he.

And same to you, Son.

I don't know why I called him Son. Well, one way or

7

another they're all our sons. The only requirement is that they be younger than us. But then again, Traynor seemed to be aging by the minute.

You looks tired, I said. Come on in and have a glass of Christmas cheer.

J. T. ain't never in his life been able to act decent to a white man he wasn't working for, but he poured Traynor a glass of bourbon and water, then he took all the children and grandkids and friends and whatnot out to the den. After while I heard Traynor's voice singing the song, coming from the stereo console. It was just the kind of Christmas present my kids would consider cute.

I looked at Traynor, complicit. But he looked like it was the last thing in the world he wanted to hear. His head was pitched forward over his lap, his hands holding his glass and his elbows on his knees.

I done sung that song seem like a million times this year, he said. I sung it on the Grand Ole Opry, I sung it on the Ed Sullivan show. I sung it on Mike Douglas, I sung it at the Cotton Bowl, the Orange Bowl. I sung it at Festivals. I sung it at Fairs. I sung it overseas in Rome, Italy, and once in a submarine *underseas.* I've sung it and sung it, and I'm making forty thousand dollars a day offa it, and you know what, I don't have the faintest notion what that song means.

Whatchumean, what do it mean? It mean what it says. All I could think was: These suckers is making forty thousand a *day* offa my song and now they gonna come back and try to swindle me out of the original thousand.

It's just a song, I said. Cagey. When you fool around with a lot of no count mens you sing a bunch of 'em. I shrugged.

Oh, he said. Well. He started brightening up. I just come by to tell you I think you are a great singer.

He didn't blush, saying that. Just said it straight out.

And I brought you a little Christmas present too. Now

8

you take this little box and you hold it until I drive off. Then you take it outside under that first streetlight back up the street aways in front of that green house. Then you open the box and see . . . Well, just *see*.

What had come over this boy, I wondered, holding the box. I looked out the window in time to see another white man come up and get in the car with him and then two more cars full of white mens start out behind him. They was all in long black cars that looked like a funeral procession.

Little Mama, Little Mama, what it is? One of my grandkids come running up and started pulling at the box. It was wrapped in gay Christmas paper—the thick, rich kind that it's hard to picture folks making just to throw away.

J. T. and the rest of the crowd followed me out the house, up the street to the streetlight and in front of the green house. Nothing was there but somebody's gold-grilled white Cadillac. Brandnew and most distracting. We got to looking at it so till I almost forgot the little box in my hand. While the others were busy making 'miration I carefully took off the paper and ribbon and folded them up and put them in my pants pocket. What should I see but a pair of genuine solid gold caddy keys.

Dangling the keys in front of everybody's nose, I unlocked the caddy, motioned for J.T. to git in on the other side, and us didn't come back home for two days.

1960

Well, the boy was sure nuff famous by now. He was still a mite shy of twenty but already they was calling him the Emperor of Rock and Roll.

Then what should happen but the draft.

Well, says J. T. There goes all this Emperor of Rock and Roll business.

But even in the army the womens was on him like white on rice. We watched it on the News.

Dear Gracie Mae [he wrote from Germany],

*How you? Fine I hope as this leaves me doing real well.
Before I come in the army I was gaining a lot of weight and
gitting jittery from making all them dumb movies. But now
I exercise and eat right and get plenty of rest. I'm more
awake than I been in ten years.*

I wonder if you are writing any more songs?

Sincerely,
Traynor

I wrote him back:

Dear Son,

*We is all fine in the Lord's good grace and hope this finds
you the same. J. T. and me be out all times of the day and
night in that car you give me—which you know you didn't
have to do. Oh, and I do appreciate the mink and the new
self-cleaning oven. But if you send anymore stuff to eat
from Germany I'm going to have to open up a store in the
neighborhood just to get rid of it. Really, we have more
than enough of everything. The Lord is good to us and we
don't know Want.*

*Glad to here you is well and gitting your right rest. There
ain't nothing like exercising to help that along. J. T. and
me work some part of every day that we don't go fishing in
the garden.*

Well, so long Soldier.

Sincerely,
Gracie Mae

He wrote:

Dear Gracie Mae,

*I hope you and J. T. like that automatic power tiller I
had one of the stores back home send you. I went through*

10

*a mountain of catalogs looking for it—I wanted something
that even a woman could use.*

*I've been thinking about writing some songs of my own
but every time I finish one it don't seem to be about nothing I've actually lived myself. My agent keeps sending me
other people's songs but they just sound mooney. I can
hardly git through 'em without gagging.*

*Everybody still loves that song of yours. They ask me all
the time what do I think it means, really. I mean, they want
to know just what I want to know. Where out of your life
did it come from?*

Sincerely,
Traynor

1968

I didn't see the boy for seven years. No. Eight. Because
just about everybody was dead when I saw him again.
Malcolm X, King, the president and his brother, and
even J. T. J. T. died of a head cold. It just settled in his
head like a block of ice, he said, and nothing we did moved
it until one day he just leaned out the bed and died.

His good friend Horace helped me put him away, and
then about a year later Horace and me started going together. We was sitting out on the front porch swing one
summer night, dusk-dark, and I saw this great procession
of lights winding to a stop.

Holy Toledo! said Horace. (He's got a real sexy voice
like Ray Charles.) Look *at* it. He meant the long line of
flashy cars and the white men in white summer suits
jumping out on the drivers' sides and standing at attention. With wings they could pass for angels, with hoods
they could be the Klan.

Traynor comes waddling up the walk.

And suddenly I know what it is he could pass for. An
Arab like the ones you see in storybooks. Plump and soft

and with never a care about weight. Because with so much money, who cares? Traynor is almost dressed like someone from a storybook too. He has on, I swear, about ten necklaces. Two sets of bracelets on his arms, at least one ring on every finger, and some kind of shining buckles on his shoes, so that when he walks you get quite a few twinkling lights.

Gracie Mae, he says, coming up to give me a hug. J. T.

I explain that J. T. passed. That this is Horace.

Horace, he says, puzzled but polite, sort of rocking back on his heels, Horace.

That's it for Horace. He goes in the house and don't come back.

Looks like you and me is gained a few, I say.

He laughs. The first time I ever heard him laugh. It don't sound much like a laugh and I can't swear that it's better than no laugh a'tall.

He's gitting fat for sure, but he's still slim compared to me. I'll never see three hundred pounds again and I've just about said (excuse me) fuck it. I got to thinking about it one day an' I thought: aside from the fact that they say it's unhealthy, my fat ain't never been no trouble. Mens always have loved me. My kids ain't never complained. Plus they's fat. And fat like I is I looks distinguished. You see me coming and know somebody's *there*.

Gracie Mae, he says, I've come with a personal invitation to you to my house tomorrow for dinner. He laughed. What did it sound like? I couldn't place it. See them men out there? he asked me. I'm sick and tired of eating with them. They don't never have nothing to talk about. That's why I eat so much. But if you come to dinner tomorrow we can talk about the old days. You can tell me about that farm I bought you.

I sold it, I said.

You did?

Yeah, I said, I did. Just cause I said I liked to exercise

by working in a garden didn't mean I wanted five hundred acres! Anyhow, I'm a city girl now. Raised in the country it's true. Dirt poor—the whole bit—but that's all behind me now.

Oh well, he said, I didn't mean to offend you.

We sat a few minutes listening to the crickets.

Then he said: You wrote that song while you was still on the farm, didn't you, or was it right after you left?

You had somebody spying on me? I asked.

You and Bessie Smith got into a fight over it once, he said.

You *is* been spying on me!

But I don't know what the fight was about, he said. Just like I don't know what happened to your second husband. Your first one died in the Texas electric chair. Did you know that? Your third one beat you up, stole your touring costumes and your car and retired with a chorine to Tuskegee. He laughed. He's still there.

I had been mad, but suddenly I calmed down. Traynor was talking very dreamily. It was dark but seems like I could tell his eyes weren't right. It was like some*thing* was sitting there talking to me but not necessarily with a person behind it.

You gave up on marrying and seem happier for it. He laughed again. I married but it never went like it was supposed to. I never could squeeze any of my own life either into it or out of it. It was like singing somebody else's record. I copied the way it was sposed to be *exactly* but I never had a clue what marriage meant.

I bought her a diamond ring big as your fist. I bought her clothes. I built her a mansion. But right away she didn't want the boys to stay there. Said they smoked up the bottom floor. Hell, there were *five* floors.

No need to grieve, I said. No need to. Plenty more where she come from.

He perked up. That's part of what that song means, ain't

it? No need to grieve. Whatever it is, there's plenty more down the line.

I never really believed that way back when I wrote that song, I said. It was all bluffing then. The trick is to live long enough to put your young bluffs to use. Now if I was to sing that song today I'd tear it up. 'Cause I done lived long enough to know it's *true*. Them words could hold me up.

I ain't lived that long, he said.

Look like you on your way, I said. I don't know why, but the boy seemed to need some encouraging. And I don't know, seem like one way or another you talk to rich white folks and you end up reassuring *them*. But what the hell, by now I feel something for the boy. I wouldn't be in his bed all alone in the middle of the night for nothing. Couldn't be nothing worse than being famous the world over for something you don't even understand. That's what I tried to tell Bessie. She wanted that same song. Overheard me practicing it one day, said, with her hands on her hips: Gracie Mae, I'ma sing your song tonight. I *likes* it.

Your lips be too swole to sing, I said. She was mean and she was strong, but I trounced her.

Ain't you famous enough with your own stuff? I said. Leave mine alone. Later on, she thanked me. By then she was Miss Bessie Smith to the World, and I was still Miss Gracie Mae Nobody from Notasulga.

The next day all these limousines arrived to pick me up. Five cars and twelve bodyguards. Horace picked that morning to start painting the kitchen.

Don't paint the kitchen, fool, I said. The only reason that dumb boy of ours is going to show me his mansion is because he intends to present us with a new house.

What you gonna do with it? he asked me, standing there in his shirtsleeves stirring the paint.

14

Sell it. Give it to the children. Live in it on weekends. It don't matter what I do. He sure don't care.

Horace just stood there shaking his head. Mama you sure looks *good*, he says. Wake me up when you git back.

Fool, I say, and pat my wig in front of the mirror.

The boy's house is something else. First you come to this mountain, and then you commence to drive and drive up this road that's lined with magnolias. Do magnolias grow on mountains? I was wondering. And you come to lakes and you come to ponds and you come to deer and you come up on some sheep. And I figure these two is sposed to represent England and Wales. Or something out of Europe. And you just keep on coming to stuff. And it's all pretty. Only the man driving my car don't look at nothing but the road. Fool. And then *finally*, after all this time, you begin to go up the driveway. And there's more magnolias—only they're not in such good shape. It's sort of cool up this high and I don't think they're gonna make it. And then I see this building that looks like if it had a name it would be The Tara Hotel. Columns and steps and outdoor chandeliers and rocking chairs. Rocking chairs? Well, and there's the boy on the steps dressed in a dark green satin jacket like you see folks wearing on TV late at night, and he looks sort of like a fat dracula with all that house rising behind him, and standing beside him there's this little white vision of loveliness that he introduces as his wife.

He's nervous when he introduces us and he says to her: This is Gracie Mae Still, I want you to know me. I mean . . . and she gives him a look that would fry meat.

Won't you come in, Gracie Mae, she says, and that's the last I see of her.

He fishes around for something to say or do and decides to escort me to the kitchen. We go through the entry and the parlor and the breakfast room and the dining room

15

and the servants' passage and finally get there. The first thing I notice is that, altogether, there are five stoves. He looks about to introduce me to one.

Wait a minute, I say. Kitchens don't do nothing for me. Let's go sit on the front porch.

Well, we hike back and we sit in the rocking chairs rocking until dinner.

Gracie Mae, he says down the table, taking a piece of fried chicken from the woman standing over him, I got a little surprise for you.

It's a house, ain't it? I ask, spearing a chitlin.

You're getting *spoiled*, he says. And the way he says *spoiled* sounds funny. He slurs it. It sounds like his tongue is too thick for his mouth. Just that quick he's finished the chicken and is now eating chitlins *and* a pork chop. *Me* spoiled, I'm thinking.

I already got a house. Horace is right this minute painting the kitchen. I bought that house. My kids feel comfortable in that house.

But this one I bought you is just like mine. Only a little smaller.

I still don't need no house. And anyway who would clean it?

He looks surprised.

Really, I think, some peoples advance *so* slowly.

I hadn't thought of that. But what the hell, I'll get you somebody to live in.

I don't want other folks living 'round me. Makes me nervous.

You *don't?* It *do?*

What I want to wake up and see folks I don't even know for?

He just sits there downtable staring at me. Some of that feeling is in the song, ain't it? Not the words, the *feeling*. What I want to wake up and see folks I don't even know for? But I see twenty folks a day I don't even know, including my wife.

This food wouldn't be bad to wake up to though, I said. The boy had found the genius of corn bread.

He looked at me real hard. He laughed. Short. They want what you got but they don't want you. They want what I got only it ain't mine. That's what makes 'em so hungry for me when I sing. They getting the flavor of something but they ain't getting the thing itself. They like a pack of hound dogs trying to gobble up a scent.

You talking 'bout your fans?

Right. Right. He says.

Don't worry 'bout your fans, I say. They don't know their asses from a hole in the ground. I doubt there's a honest one in the bunch.

That's the point. Dammit, that's the point! He hits the table with his fist. It's so solid it don't even quiver. You need a honest audience! You can't have folks that's just gonna lie right back to you.

Yeah, I say, it was small compared to yours, but I had one. It would have been worth my life to try to sing 'em somebody else's stuff that I didn't know nothing about.

He must have pressed a buzzer under the table. One of his flunkies zombies up.

Git Johnny Carson, he says.

On the phone? asks the zombie.

On the phone, says Traynor, what you think I mean, git him offa the front porch? Move your ass.

So two weeks later we's on the Johnny Carson show.

Traynor is all corseted down nice and looks a little bit fat but mostly good. And all the women that grew up on him and my song squeal and squeal. Traynor says: The lady who wrote my first hit record is here with us tonight, and she's agreed to sing it for all of us, just like she sung it forty-five years ago. Ladies and Gentlemen, the great Gracie Mae Still!

Well, I had tried to lose a couple of pounds my own self, but failing that I had me a very big dress made. So I sort of rolls over next to Traynor, who is dwarfted by me, so that when he puts his arm around back of me to try to hug me it looks funny to the audience and they laugh.

I can see this pisses him off. But I smile out there at 'em. Imagine squealing for twenty years and not knowing why you're squealing? No more sense of endings and beginnings than hogs.

It don't matter, Son, I say. Don't fret none over me.

I commence to sing. And I sound —— wonderful. Being able to sing good ain't all about having a good singing voice a'tall. A good singing voice helps. But when you come up in the Hard Shell Baptist church like I did you understand early that the fellow that sings is the singer. Them that waits for programs and arrangements and letters from home is just good voices occupying body space.

So there I am singing my own song, my own way. And I give it all I got and enjoy every minute of it. When I finish Traynor is standing up clapping and clapping and beaming at first me and then the audience like I'm his mama for true. The audience claps politely for about two seconds.

Traynor looks disgusted.

He comes over and tries to hug me again. The audience laughs.

Johnny Carson looks at us like we both weird.

Traynor is mad as hell. He's supposed to sing something called a love ballad. But instead he takes the mike, turns to me and says: Now see if my imitation still holds up. He goes into the same song, *our* song, I think, looking out at his flaky audience. And he sings it just the way he always did. My voice, my tone, my inflection, everything. But he forgets a couple of lines. Even before he's finished the matronly squeals begin.

He sits down next to me looking whipped.

It don't matter, Son, I say, patting his hand. You don't even know those people. Try to make the people you know happy.

Is that in the song? he asks.

Maybe. I say.

1977

For a few years I hear from him, then nothing. But trying to lose weight takes all the attention I got to spare. I finally faced up to the fact that my fat is the hurt I don't admit, not even to myself, and that I been trying to bury it from the day I was born. But also when you git real old, to tell the truth, it ain't as pleasant. It gits lumpy and slack. Yuck. So one day I said to Horace, I'ma git this shit offa me.

And he fell in with the program like he always try to do and Lord such a procession of salads and cottage cheese and fruit juice!

One night I dreamed Traynor had split up with his fifteenth wife. He said: *You meet 'em for no reason. You date 'em for no reason. You marry 'em for no reason. I do it all but I swear it's just like somebody else doing it. I feel like I can't remember Life.*

The boy's in trouble, I said to Horace.

You've always said that, he said.

I have?

Yeah. You always said he looked asleep. You can't sleep through life if you wants to live it.

You not such a fool after all, I said, pushing myself up with my cane and hobbling over to where he was. Let me sit down on your lap, I said, while this salad I ate takes effect.

In the morning we heard Traynor was dead. Some said

19

fat, some said heart, some said alcohol, some said drugs. One of the children called from Detroit. Them dumb fans of his is on a crying rampage, she said. You just ought to turn on the t.v.

But I didn't want to see 'em. They was crying and crying and didn't even know what they was crying for. One day this is going to be a pitiful country, I thought.

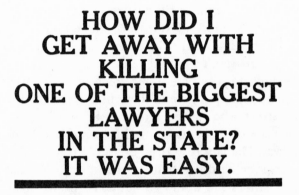

HOW DID I
GET AWAY WITH
KILLING
ONE OF THE BIGGEST
LAWYERS
IN THE STATE?
IT WAS EASY.

"My mother and father were not married. I never knew him. My mother must have loved him, though; she never talked against him when I was little. It was like he never existed. We lived on Poultry street. Why it was called Poultry street I never knew. I guess at one time there must have been a chicken factory somewhere along there. It was right near the center of town. I could walk to the state capitol in less than ten minutes. I could see the top —it was gold—of the capitol building from the front yard. When I was a little girl I used to think it was real gold, shining up there, and then they bought an eagle and put him on top, and when I used to walk up there I couldn't see the top of the building from the ground, it was so high, and I used to reach down and run my hand over the grass. It was like a rug, that grass was, so springy and silky and deep. They had these big old trees, too. Oaks and magnolias; and I thought the magnolia trees were beautiful and one night I climbed up in one of them and got a bloom and took it home. But the air in our house blighted it; it turned brown the minute I took it inside and the petals dropped off.

"Mama worked in private homes. That's how she described her job, to make it sound nicer. 'I work in private homes,' she would say, and that sounded nicer, she thought, than saying 'I'm a maid.'

"Sometimes she made six dollars a day, working in two private homes. Most of the time she didn't make that much. By the time she paid the rent and bought milk and bananas there wasn't anything left.

"She used to leave me alone sometimes because there was no one to keep me—and then there was an old woman up the street who looked after me for a while—and by the time she died she was more like a mother to me than Mama was. Mama was so tired every night when she came home I never hardly got the chance to talk to her. And then sometimes she would go out at night, or bring men home—but they never thought of marrying her. And they sure didn't want to be bothered with me. I guess most of them were like my own father; had children somewhere of their own that they'd left. And then they came to my Mama, who fell for them every time. And I think she may have had a couple of abortions, like some of the women did, who couldn't feed any more mouths. But she tried.

"Anyway, she was a nervous kind of woman. I think she had spells or something because she was so tired. But I didn't understand anything then about exhaustion, worry, lack of a proper diet; I just thought she wanted to work, to be away from the house. I didn't blame her. Where we lived people sometimes just threw pieces of furniture they didn't want over the railing. And there was broken glass and rags everywhere. The place stunk, especially in the summer. And children were always screaming and men were always cussing and women were always yelling about something. . . . It was nothing for a girl or woman to be raped. I was raped myself, when I was twelve, and my Mama never knew and I never told anybody. For, what could they do? It was just a boy, passing through. Somebody's cousin from the North.

"One time my Mama was doing day's work at a private home and took me with her. It was like being in fairyland. Everything was spotless and new, even before Mama started cleaning. I met the woman in the house and played with her children. I didn't even see the man, but he was in there somewhere, while I was out in the yard with the children. I was fourteen, but I guess I looked like a grown woman. Or maybe I looked fourteen. Anyway, the next day, he picked me up when I was coming from school and he said my Mama had asked him to do it. I got in the car with him . . . he took me to his law office, a big office in the middle of town, and he started asking me questions about 'how do you all live?' and 'what grade are you in?' and stuff like that. And then he began to touch me, and I pulled away. But he kept touching me and I was scared . . . he raped me. But afterward he told me he hadn't forced me, that I felt something for him, and he gave me some money. I was crying, going down the stairs. I wanted to kill him.

"I never told Mama. I thought that would be the end of it. But about two days later, on my way from school, he stopped his car again, and I got in. This time we went to his house; nobody was there. And he made me get into his wife's bed. After we'd been doing this for about three weeks, he told me he loved me. I didn't love him, but he had begun to look a little better to me. Really, I think, because he was so clean. He bathed a lot and never smelled even alive, to tell the truth. Or maybe it was the money he gave me, or the presents he bought. I told Mama I had a job after school baby-sitting. And she was glad that I could buy things I needed for school. But it was all from him.

"This went on for two years. He wouldn't let me get pregnant, he said, and I didn't. I would just lay up there in his wife's bed and work out algebra problems or think about what new thing I was going to buy. But one day, when I got home, Mama was there ahead of me, and she saw me get out of his car. I knew when he was driving off that I was going to get it.

"Mama asked me didn't I know he was a white man? Didn't I know he was a married man with two children? Didn't I have good sense? And do you know what I told her? *I told her he loved me.* Mama was crying and praying at the same time by then. The neighbors heard both of us screaming and crying, because Mama beat me almost to death with the cord from the electric iron. She just hacked it off the iron, still on the ironing board. She beat me till she couldn't raise her arm. And then she had one of her fits, just twitching and sweating and trying to claw herself into the floor. This scared me more than the beating. That night she told me something I hadn't paid much attention to before. She said: 'On top of everything else, that man's daddy goes on the t.v. every night and says folks like us ain't even human.' It was his daddy who had stood in the schoolhouse door saying it would be over his dead body before any black children would come into a white school.

"But do you think that stopped me? No. I would look at his daddy on t.v. ranting and raving about how integration was a communist plot, and I would just think of how different his son Bubba was from his daddy! Do you understand what I'm saying. I thought he *loved* me. That *meant* something to me. What did I know about 'equal rights'? What did I care about 'integration'? I was sixteen! I wanted somebody to tell me I was pretty, and he was telling me that all the time. I even thought it was *brave* of him to go with me. History? What did I know about History?

"I began to hate Mama. We argued about Bubba all the time, for months. And I still slipped out to meet him, because Mama had to work. I told him how she beat me, and about how much she despised him—he was really pissed off that any black person could despise him—and about how she had these spells. . . . Well, the day I became seventeen, the *day* of my seventeenth birthday, I signed papers in his law office, and I had my mother committed to an insane asylum.

"After Mama had been in Carthage Insane Asylum for three months, she managed somehow to get a lawyer. An old slick-headed man who smoked great big black cigars. People laughed at him because he didn't even have a law office, but he was the only lawyer that would touch the case, because Bubba's daddy was such a big deal. And we all gathered in the judge's chambers—because he wasn't about to let this case get out. Can you imagine, if it had? And Mama's old lawyer told the judge how Bubba's daddy had tried to buy him off. And Bubba got up and swore he'd never touched me. And then I got up and said Mama was insane. And do you know what? By that time it was true. Mama *was* insane. She had no mind left at all. They had given her shock treatments or something. . . . God knows what else they gave her. But she was as vacant as an empty eye socket. She just sat sort of hunched over, and her hair was white.

"And after all this, Bubba wanted us to keep going together. Mama was just an obstacle that he felt he had removed. But I just suddenly—in a way I don't even pretend to understand—woke up. It was like everything up to then had been some kind of dream. And I told him I wanted to get Mama out. But he wouldn't do it; he just kept trying to make me go with him. And sometimes—out of habit, I guess—I did. My body did what it was being paid to do. And Mama died. And I killed Bubba.

"How did I get away with killing one of the biggest lawyers in the state? It was easy. He kept a gun in his desk drawer at the office and one night I took it out and shot him. I shot him while he was wearing his thick winter overcoat, so I wouldn't have to see him bleed. But I don't think I took the time to wipe off my fingerprints, because, to tell the truth, I couldn't stand it another minute in that place. No one came after me, and I read in the paper the next day that he'd been killed by burglars. I guess they thought 'burglars' had stolen all that money Bubba kept in his safe—but I had it. One of the carrots Bubba always dangled before me was that he was going to send me to college: I didn't see why he shouldn't do it.

"The strangest thing was, Bubba's wife came over to the house and asked me if I'd mind looking after the children while she went to Bubba's funeral. I did it, of course, because I was afraid she'd suspect something if I didn't. So on the day he was buried I was in his house, sitting on his wife's bed with his children, and eating fried chicken his wife, Julie, had cooked."

ELETHIA

*A certain perverse experience shaped Elethia's life, and
made it possible for it to be true that she carried with her
at all times a small apothecary jar of ashes.*

*There was in the town where she was born a man whose
ancestors had owned a large plantation on which everything under the sun was made or grown. There had been
many slaves, and though slavery no longer existed, this
grandson of former slaveowners held a quaint proprietary
point of view where colored people were concerned. He
adored them, of course. Not in the present—it went without saying—but at that time, stopped, just on the outskirts
of his memory: his grandfather's time.*

*This man, whom Elethia never saw, opened a locally
famous restaurant on a busy street near the center of town.
He called it "Old Uncle Albert's." In the window of the
restaurant was a stuffed likeness of Uncle Albert himself,*

a small brown dummy of waxen skin and glittery black eyes. His lips were intensely smiling and his false teeth shone. He carried a covered tray in one hand, raised level with his shoulder, and over his other arm was draped a white napkin.

Black people could not eat at Uncle Albert's, though they worked, of course, in the kitchen. But on Saturday afternoons a crowd of them would gather to look at "Uncle Albert" and discuss how near to the real person the dummy looked. Only the very old people remembered Albert Porter, and their eyesight was no better than their memory. Still there was a comfort somehow in knowing that Albert's likeness was here before them daily and that if he smiled as a dummy in a fashion he was not known to do as a man, well, perhaps both memory and eyesight were wrong.

The old people appeared grateful to the rich man who owned the restaurant for giving them a taste of vicarious fame. They could pass by the gleaming window where Uncle Albert stood, seemingly in the act of sprinting forward with his tray, and know that though niggers were not allowed in the front door, ole Albert was already inside, and looking mighty pleased about it, too.

For Elethia the fascination was in Uncle Albert's fingernails. She wondered how his creator had got them on. She wondered also about the white hair that shone so brightly under the lights. One summer she worked as a salad girl in the restaurant's kitchen, and it was she who discovered the truth about Uncle Albert. He was not a dummy; he was stuffed. Like a bird, like a moose's head, like a giant bass. He was stuffed.

One night after the restaurant was closed someone broke in and stole nothing but Uncle Albert. It was Elethia and her friends, boys who were in her class and who called her "Thia." Boys who bought Thunderbird and shared it with her. Boys who laughed at her jokes so much they hardly *remembered she was also cute. Her tight buddies. They carefully burned Uncle Albert to ashes in the incinerator of their high school, and each of them kept a bottle of his ashes. And for each of them what they knew and their reaction to what they knew was profound.*

The experience undercut whatever solid foundation Elethia had assumed she had. She became secretive, wary, looking over her shoulder at the slightest noise. She haunted the museums of any city in which she found herself, looking, usually, at the remains of Indians, for they were plentiful everywhere she went. She discovered some of the Indian warriors and maidens in the museums were also real, stuffed people, painted and wigged and robed, like figures in the Rue Morgue. There were so many, in fact, that she could not possibly steal and burn them all. Besides, she did not know if these figures—with their valiant glass eyes—would wish to be burned.

About Uncle Albert she felt she knew.

What kind of man was Uncle Albert?

Well, the old folks said, he wasn't nobody's uncle and wouldn't sit still for nobody to call him that, either.

Why, said another old-timer, I recalls the time they hung a boy's privates on a post at the end of the street where all the black folks shopped, just to scare us all, you understand, and Albert Porter was the one took 'em down and buried 'em. Us never did find the rest of the boy though. It was just like always—they would throw you in the river with a big old green log tied to you, and down to the bottom you sunk.

He continued:

Albert was born in slavery and he remembered that his mama and daddy didn't know nothing about slavery'd done ended for near 'bout ten years, the boss man kept them so ignorant of the law, you understand. So he was a mad so-an'-so when he found out. They used to beat him severe *trying to make him forget the past and grin and act like a nigger. (Whenever you saw somebody acting like a nigger, Albert said, you could be sure he seriously disremembered his past.) But he never would. Never would work in the big house as head servant, neither—always broke up stuff. The master at that time was always going around pinching him too. Looks like he hated Albert more than anything —but he never would let him get a job anywhere else. And Albert never would leave home. Too stubborn.*

Stubborn, yes. My land, another one said. That's why it do seem strange to see that dummy that sposed to be ole Albert with his mouth open. All them teeth. Hell, all Albert's teeth was knocked out before he was grown.

Elethia went away to college and her friends went into the army because they were poor and that was the way things were. They discovered Uncle Alberts all over the world. Elethia was especially disheartened to find Uncle Alberts in her textbooks, in the newspapers and on t.v.

Everywhere she looked there was an Uncle Albert (and many Aunt Albertas, it goes without saying).

But she had her jar of ashes, the old-timers' memories written down, and her friends who wrote that in the army they were learning skills that would get them through more than a plate glass window.

And she was careful that, no matter how compelling the hype, Uncle Alberts, in her own mind, were not permitted to exist.

THE LOVER

For Joanne

Her husband had wanted a child and so she gave him one as a gift, because she liked her husband and admired him greatly. Still, it had taken a lot out of her, especially in the area of sexual response. She had never been particularly passionate with him, not even during the early years of their marriage; it was more a matter of being sexually comfortable. After the birth of the child she simply never thought of him sexually at all. She supposed their marriage was better than most, even so. He was a teacher at a University near their home in the Midwest and cared about his students—which endeared him to her, who had had so many uncaring teachers; and toward her own work, which was poetry (that she set very successfully to jazz), he showed the utmost understanding and respect.

31

She was away for two months at an artists' colony in New England and that is where she met Ellis, whom she immediately dubbed, once she had got over thinking he resembled (with his top lip slightly raised over his right eyetooth when he smiled) a wolf, "The Lover." They met one evening before dinner as she was busy ignoring the pompous bullshit of a fellow black poet, a man many years older than she who had no concept of other people's impatience. He had been rambling on about himself for over an hour and she had at first respectfully listened because she was the kind of person whose adult behavior—in a situation like this—reflected her childhood instruction; and she was instructed as a child, to be polite.

She was always getting herself stuck in one-sided conversations of this sort because she was—the people who talked to her seemed to think—an excellent listener. She was, up to a point. She was genuinely interested in older artists in particular and would sit, entranced, as they spun out their tales of art and lust (the gossip, though old, was delicious!) of forty years ago.

But there had been only a few of these artists whose tales she had listened to until the end. For as soon as a note of bragging entered into the conversation—a famous name dropped here, an expensive Paris restaurant's menu dropped there, and especially the names of the old artist's neglected books and on what occasion the wretched creature had insulted this or that weasel of a white person—her mind began to turn about upon itself until it rolled out some of her own thoughts to take the place of the trash that was coming in.

And so it was on that evening before dinner. The old poet—whose work was exceedingly mediocre, and whose only attractions, as far as she was concerned, were his age and his rather bitter wit—fastened his black, bloodshot eyes upon her (in which she read desperation and a prayer of unstrenuous seduction) and held her to a close atten-

32

tion to his words. Except that she had perfected the trick—as had many of her contemporaries who hated to be rude and who, also, had a strong sense of self-preservation (because the old poet, though, she thought, approaching senility, was yet a powerful figure in black literary circles and thought nothing of using his considerable influence to thwart the careers of younger talents)—of keeping her face quite animated and turned full onto the speaker, while inside her head she could be trying out the shades of paint with which to improve the lighting of her house. In fact, so intense did her concentration appear, it seemed she read the speaker's lips.

Ellis, who would be her lover, had come into the room and sat down on a chair by the fire. For although it was the middle of summer, a fire was needed against the chilly New England evenings.

"Have you been waiting long?" he asked.

And it suddenly occurred to her that indeed she had.

"But of course," she answered absently, noting the crooked smile that reminded her of a snarling, though not disagreeable, wolf—and turned back just as the old poet jealously reached out his hand to draw her attention to the, for him, hilarious ending of his story. She laughed and slapped her knee, a gesture of such fraudulent folksiness that she was soon laughing in earnest. Catching Ellis's eye as she thus amused herself she noticed therein a particular gleam that she instantly recognized.

"My lover," she thought, noticing for the first time his head of blue-black curls, his eyes as brown as the Mississippi, his skin that was not as successfully tanned as it might have been but which would definitely do. He was thin and tall, with practically no hips in the beige twill jeans he wore.

At dinner they sat together, looking out at the blue New England mountains in the distance, as the sun left tracings of orange and pink against the pale blue sky. He had heard she'd won some sort of prize—a prestigious one—for her "jazzed-up" poetry, and the way he said it made her glance critically at his long fingers wrapped around his wine glass. She wondered if they would be as sensitive on her skin as they looked. She had never heard of him, though she did not say so, probably because he had already said it for her. He talked a good deal—easily and early—about himself, and she was quite relaxed—even entertained—in her listener's role.

He wondered what, *if anything*, younger poets like herself had to say, since he was of the opinion that not much was learned about life until the middle years. He was in his forties. Of course he didn't look it, but he was much older than she, he said, and the reason that he was not better known was because he could not find a publisher for his two novels (still, by the way, unpublished—in case she knew publishers) or for his poetry, which an acquaintance of his had compared to something or other by Montaigne.

"You're lovely," he said into the brief silence.

"And you seem bright," she automatically replied.

She had blocked him out since his mention of the two unpublished novels. By the time he began complaining about the preferential treatment publishers now gave minorities and women she was on the point of yawning or gazing idly about the room. But she did not do either for a very simple reason: when she had first seen him she had thought—after the wolf thing—"my lover," and had liked, deep down inside, the illicit sound of it. She had never had a lover; he would be her first. Afterwards, she would be truly a woman of her time. She also responded to his curly hair and slim, almost nonexistent hips, in a surprisingly passionate way.

She was a woman who, after many tribulations in her life, few of which she ever discussed even with close friends, had reached the point of being generally pleased with herself. This self-acceptance was expressed in her eyes,

34

which were large, dark and clear and which, more often
than not, seemed predisposed to smile. Though not tall,
her carriage gave the illusion of height, as did her carefully
selected tall sandals and her naturally tall hair, which stood
in an elegant black afro with exactly seven strands of silver
hair—of which she was very proud (she was just thirty-one)
—shining across the top. She wore long richly colored
skirts that—when she walked—parted without warning
along the side, and exposed a flash of her creamy brown
thigh, and legs that were curvaceous and strong. If she
came late to the dining room and stood in the doorway a
moment longer than necessary—looking about for a place
to sit after she had her tray—for that moment the noise
from the cutlery already in use was still.

What others minded at the Colony—whether too many
frogs in the frog pond (which was used for swimming) or
not enough wine with the veal (there was talk of cutting
out wine with meals altogether, and thereby ending a fine
old Colony tradition!)—she did not seem to mind. She
seemed open, bright, occasionally preoccupied, but always
ready with an appreciative ear, or at times a humorous, if
outdated joke of her own (which she nevertheless told with
gusto and found funny herself, because she would laugh
and laugh at it, regardless of what her listeners did). She
seemed never to strain over her work, and literally never
complained about its progress—or lack thereof. It was as
if she worked only for herself, for her own enjoyment (or
salvation) and was—whether working or simply thinking
of working—calm about it.

Even the distraction caused by the birth of her child
was a price she was, ultimately, prepared to pay. She did
not intend to have a second one, after all—that would be
too stupid—and this one would, before she knew it, be
grown up enough for boarding school.

Relishing her short freedom during the summer as much
as she contemplated enjoyment of her longer future one,

she threw herself headlong into the interim relationship with Ellis, a professional lover of mainly older women artists who came to the Colony every year to work and play.

A New York Jew of considerable charm, intellectual pettiness, and so vast and uncritical a love of all things European it struck one as an illness (and who hated Brooklyn—where he had grown up—his parents, Jewish culture, and all he had observed of black behavior in New York City), Ellis found the listening silence of "the dark woman," as he euphemistically called her, restorative—after his endless evenings with talkative women who wrote for *Esquire* and the *New York Times*. Such women made it possible for him to be included in the proper tennis sets and swimming parties at the Colony—in which he hoped to meet contacts who would help his career along —but they were also driven to examine each and every one of their own thoughts aloud. His must be the attentive ear, since they had already "made it" and were comfortable exposing their own charming foibles to him, while he, not having made it yet, could afford to expose nothing that might discourage their assistance in his behalf.

It amused and thrilled him to almost hear the "click" when his eyes met those of the jazz poet. "Sex," he thought. And, "rest."

Of course he mistook her intensity.

After sitting before her piano for hours, setting one of her poems to music, she would fling open her cabin door and wave to him as he walked by on his way to or from the lake. He was writing a novella about his former wife and composed it in longhand down at the lake ("So if I get fed up with it I can toss myself in," he joked) and then took it back to his studio with him to type. She would call to him, her hair and clothing very loose, and entice him into her cabin with promises of sympathy and half her lunch.

When they made love she was disappointed. He did not appear to believe in unhurried pleasure, and thought the things she suggested he might do to please her very awkward at the least. But it hardly mattered, since what mattered was the fact of having a lover. She liked snuggling up to him, liked kissing him along the sides of his face— his cheeks were just beginning to be a trifle flabby but would still be good for several years—and loved to write him silly letters—scorching with passion and promises of abandon—that made her seem head over heels in love. She enjoyed writing the letters because she enjoyed feeling to her full capacity and for as long as possible the excitement having a lover brought. It was the kind of excitement she'd felt years ago, in high school and perhaps twice in college (once when she'd fallen for a student and once when she was seduced—with her help and consent—by a teacher), and she recognized it as a feeling to be enjoyed for all it was worth. Her body felt on fire, her heart jumped in her breast, her pulse raced—she was aware, for the first time in years, of actually *needing* to make love.

He began to think he must fight her off, at least a little bit. She was too intense, he said. He did not have time for intense relationships, that's why he had finally accepted a divorce ,from his wife. He was also writing a great poem which he had begun in 1950 and which—now that he was at the Colony—he hoped to finish. She should concentrate on her own work if she expected to win any more prizes. She *wanted* to win more, didn't she?

She laughed at him, but would not tell him why. Instead she tried, very gently (while sitting on his lap with her bosom maternally opposite his face), to tell him he misunderstood. That she wanted nothing from him beyond the sensation of being in love itself. (His stare was at first blank, then cynical, at this.) As for her work, she did not do hers the way he apparently did his. Hers did not mean to her what he seemed to think it meant. It did not get in the way of her living, for example, and if it ever did, she felt sure she would remove it. Prizes were nice—especially if they brought one money (which one might then use to explore Barbados! China! Mozambique!)—but they were not rewards she could count on. Her life, on the other hand, *was* a reward she could count on. (He became impatient with this explanation and a little angry.)

It was their first quarrel.

When he saw her again she had spent the weekend (which had been coming up) in nearby Boston. She looked cheerful, happy and relaxed. From her letters to him—which he had thought embarrassingly self-revealing and erotic, though flattering, of course, to him—he had assumed she was on the point of declaring her undying love and of wanting to run away with him. Instead, she had gone off for two days, without mentioning it to him. And she had gone, so she said, by herself!

She soothed him as best she could. Lied, which she hated more than anything, about her work. "It was going so *poorly*," she complained (and the words rang metallic in her mouth); "I just couldn't bear staying here doing nothing where working conditions are so *idyllic!*" He appeared somewhat mollified. Actually, her work was going fine and she had sent off to her publishers a completed book of poems and jazz arrangements—which was what she had come to the Colony to do. "Your work was going swimmingly down at the lake," she giggled. "I didn't wish to disturb you."

And yet it was clear he was disturbed.

So she did not tell him she had flown all the way home.

He was always questioning her now about her town, her house, her child, her husband. She found herself describing her husband as if to a prospective bride. She lingered over the wiry bronze of his hair, the evenness of his teeth, his black, black eyes, the thrilling timbre of his deep voice. It *was* an exceptionally fine voice, it seemed to her now, listening to Ellis's rather whining one. Though, on second thought, it was perhaps nothing special.

At night, after a rousing but unsatisfactory evening with Ellis, she dreamed of her husband making love to her on the kitchen floor at home, where the sunlight collected in a pool beneath the window, and lay in bed next day dreaming of all the faraway countries, daring adventures, passionate lovers still to be found.

PETUNIAS

This is what they read on the next to the last page of the diary they found after her death in the explosion:

As soon as my son got off the bus from Vietnam I could tell he was different. He said, Mama, I'm going to show you how to make bombs. He went with me to the house, me thinking it was all a big joke. He had all of the stuff in a footlocker and in his duffel bag among his clothes. So it wouldn't jar, he said.

Son, I said, I don't think I want that stuff in my house.

But he just laughed. Let's make a big noise in Tranquil, Mississippi, he said.

We have always lived in Tranquil. My daddy's grandmama was a slave on the Tearslee Plantation. They dug up her grave when I started agitating in the Movement. One morning I found her dust dumped over my verbena bed, a splintery leg bone had fell among my petunias.

40

COMING APART
By Way of Introduction to Lorde, Teish and Gardner

In 1979 I was invited by Laura Lederer to write an introduction to the Third World Women's chapter of a book she was then editing about pornography called Take Back the Night. *When I agreed to write it, she sent me three essays, by Audre Lorde, Luisah Teish and Tracy A. Gardner. I was moved by the essays and the following "introduction"—published in* Ms. *before book publication simply as "A Fable"—was the result.*

The "fable" works, I think, as a story, and in fact it appears as one, rather than as an introduction, in Take Back the Night. *However, if I had written it as a story originally, making up all the parts myself, or choosing my informants, my analysis of the roots of vicious white male pornographic treatment of white women would have been somewhat different, with a longer historical perspective.*

While not denying the obvious connections between the lynching of black men and women (which, as Gardner

41

states, became prevalent only after the Civil War), and the pornographic abuse of white women, I would have argued that the more ancient roots of modern pornography are to be found in the almost always pornographic treatment of black women, who, from the moment they entered slavery, even in their own homelands, were subjected to rape as the "logical" convergence of sex and violence. Conquest, in short.

For centuries the black woman has served as the primary pornographic "outlet" for white men in Europe and America. We need only think of the black women used as breeders, raped for the pleasure and profit of their owners. We need only think of the license the "master" of the slave woman enjoyed. But, most telling of all, we need only study the old slave societies of the South to note the sadistic treatment—at the hands of white "gentlemen"—of "beautiful, young quadroons and octoroons" who became increasingly (and were deliberately bred to become) indistinguishable from white women, and were the more highly prized as slave mistresses because of this.

Although this "fable," "story," "introduction" was itself labeled pornographic and banned temporarily by at least one school district in the United States, I believe it is only by writing stories in which pornography is confronted openly and explicitly that writers can make a contribution, in their own medium, to a necessary fight.

A middle-aged husband comes home after a long day at the office. His wife greets him at the door with the news that dinner is ready. He is grateful. First, however, he must use the bathroom. In the bathroom, sitting on the commode, he opens up the *Jiveboy* magazine he has brought home in his briefcase. There are a couple of jivemate poses that particularly arouse him. He studies the young women—blonde, perhaps (the national craze), with elastic waists and inviting eyes—and strokes his penis. At the same time, his bowels stir with the desire to defecate. He is in the bathroom a luxurious ten minutes. He emerges spent, relaxed—hungry for dinner.

His wife, using the bathroom later, comes upon the slightly damp magazine. She picks it up with mixed emotions. She is a brownskin woman with black hair and eyes. She looks at the white blondes and brunettes. Will he be thinking of them, she wonders, when he is making love to me?

"Why do you need these?" she asks.

"They mean nothing," he says.

"But they hurt me somehow," she says.

"You are being a.) silly, b.) a prude, and c.) ridiculous," he says. "You know I love you."

She cannot say to him: But they are not me, those women. She cannot say she is jealous of pictures on a page. That she feels invisible. Rejected. Overlooked. She says instead, to herself: He is right. I will grow up. Adjust. Swim with the tide.

He thinks he understands her, what she has been trying to say. It is *Jiveboy*, he thinks. The white women.

Next day he brings home *Jivers*, a black magazine, filled with bronze and honey-colored women. He is in the bathroom another luxurious ten minutes.

She stands, holding the magazine: on the cover are the legs and shoes of a well-dressed black man, carrying a briefcase and a rolled *Wall Street Journal* in one hand. At his feet—she turns the magazine cover around and around to figure out how exactly the pose is accomplished—there is a woman, a brownskin woman like herself, twisted and contorted in such a way that her head is not even visible. Only her glistening body—her back and derriere—so that she looks like a human turd at the man's feet.

He is on a business trip to New York. He has brought

his wife along. He is eagerly sharing 42nd Street with her. "Look!" he says. "How *free* everything is! A far cry from Bolton!" (The small town they are from.) He is elated to see the blonde, spaced-out hookers, with their black pimps, trooping down the street. Elated at the shortness of the black hookers' dresses, their long hair, inevitably false and blond. She walks somehow behind him, so that he will encounter these wonders first. He does not notice until he turns a corner that she has stopped in front of a window that has caught her eye. While she is standing alone, looking, two separate pimps ask her what stable she is in or if in fact she is in one. Or simply "You workin'?"

He struts back and takes her elbow. Looks hard for the compliment implied in these questions, then shares it with his wife: "*You* know you're foxy!"

She is immovable. Her face suffering and wondering. "But look," she says, pointing. Four large plastic dolls— one a skinny Farrah Fawcett (or so the doll looks to her) posed for anal inspection; one, an oriental, with her eyes, strangely, closed, but her mouth, a pouting red suction cup, open; an enormous eskimo woman, with fur around her neck and ankles, and vagina; and a black woman dressed entirely in a leopard skin, complete with tail. The dolls are all life-size, and the efficiency of their rubber genitals is explained in detail on a card visible through the plate glass.

For her this is the stuff of nightmares—possibly because all the dolls are smiling. She will see them for the rest of her life. For him the sight is also shocking, but arouses a prurient curiosity. He will return, another time, alone. Meanwhile, he must prevent her from seeing such things, he resolves, whisking her briskly off the street.

Later, in their hotel room, she watches TV as two black women sing their latest hits: the first woman, dressed in a gold dress (because her song is now "solid gold!") is nonetheless wearing a chain around her ankle—the wife imagines she sees a chain—because the woman is singing: "Free me from my freedom, chain me to a tree!"

"What do you think of that?" she asks her husband.

"She's a fool," says he.

But when the second woman sings: "Ready, aim, fire, my name is desire," with guns and rockets going off all around her, he thinks the line "Shoot me with your love!" explains everything.

She is despondent.

She looks in a mirror at her plump brown and black body, crinkly hair and black eyes and decides, foolishly, that she is not beautiful. And that she is not hip, either. Among her other problems is the fact that she does not like the word "nigger" used by anyone at all, and is afraid of marijuana. These restraints, she feels, make her old, too much like her own mother, who loves sex (she has lately learned) but is highly religious and, for example, thinks cardplaying wicked and alcohol deadly. Her husband would not consider her mother sexy, she thinks. Since she herself is aging, this thought frightens her. But, surprisingly, while watching herself become her mother in the mirror, she discovers that *she* considers her mother—who carefully braids her average-length, average-grade, graying hair every night before going to bed; the braids her father still manages to fray during the night—*very* sexy.

At once she feels restored.
Resolves to fight.

"You're the only black woman in the world that worries about any of this stuff," he tells her, unaware of her resolve, and moody at her months of silent studiousness.

She says, "Here, Colored Person, read this essay by Audre Lorde."

45

He hedges. She insists.

He comes to the line about Lorde "moving into sunlight against the body of a woman I love," and bridles. "Wait a minute," he says, "what kind of a name is 'Audre' for a man? They must have meant 'And*ré*.'"

"It *is* the name of a woman," she says. "Read the rest of that page."

"No dyke can tell me anything," he says, flinging down the pages.

She has been calmly waiting for this. She brings in *Jiveboy* and *Jivers*. In both, there are women eating women they don't even know. She takes up the essay and reads:

> *This brings me to the last consideration of the erotic. To share the power of each other's feelings is different from using another's feelings as we would use Kleenex. And when we look the other way from our experience, erotic or otherwise, we use rather than share the feelings of those others who participate in the experience with us. And use without consent of the used is abuse.*

He looks at her with resentment, because she is reading this passage over again, silently, absorbedly, to herself, holding the pictures of the phony lesbians (a favorite, though unexamined, turn-on) absent-mindedly on her lap. He realizes he can never have her again sexually the way he has had her since their second year of marriage, as though her body belonged to someone else. He sees, down the road, the dissolution of the marriage, a constant search for more perfect bodies, or dumber wives. He feels oppressed by her incipient struggle, and feels somehow as if her struggle to change the pleasure he has enjoyed is a violation of his rights.

Now she is busy pasting Audre Lorde's words on the cabinet over the kitchen sink.

—

When they make love she tries to look him in the eye, but he refuses to return her gaze.

For the first time he acknowledges the awareness that the pleasure of coming without her is bitter and lonely. He thinks of eating stolen candy alone, behind the barn. And yet, he thinks greedily, it is better than nothing, which he considers her struggle's benefit to him.

The next day, she is reading another essay when he comes home from work. It is called "A Quiet Subversion," and is by Luisah Teish. "Another dyke?" he asks.

"Another one of your sisters," she replies, and begins to read, even before he's had dinner:

> *During the "Black Power Movement" much cultural education was focused on the black physique. One of the accomplishments of that period was the popularization of African hairstyles and the Natural. Along with this new hair-do came a new self-image and way of relating. Then the movie industry put out "Superfly," and the Lord Jesus Look, the Konked head, and an accompanying attitude, ran rampant in the black community. Films like "Shaft" and "Lady Sings the Blues" portray black "heroes" as cocaine-snorting, fast-life fools. In these movies a black woman is always caught in a web of violence. . . .*
>
> *A popular Berkeley theatre featured a porno movie titled "Slaves of Love." Its advertisement portrayed two black women, naked, in chains, and a white man standing over them with a whip! How such racist pornographic material escaped the eye of black activists presents a problem. . . .*

Typically, he doesn't even hear the statement about the women. "What does the bitch know about the Black Power Movement?" he fumes. He is angry at his wife for knowing him so long and so well. She knows, for instance, that because of the Black Power Movement (and really because of the Civil Rights Movement before it), and not because he was at all active in it, he holds the bourgeois job he has. She remembers when his own hair was afroed. Now it is loosely curled. It occurs to him that, because she knows him as he was, he cannot make love to her as she is. Cannot, in fact, *love* her as she is. There is a way in which, in some firmly repressed corner of his mind, he considers his wife to be *still* black, whereas he feels himself to have moved to some other plane.

(This insight, a glimmer of which occurs to him, frightens him so much that he will resist it for several years. Should he accept it at once, however unsettling, it would help him understand the illogic of his acceptance of pornography used against black women: that he has detached himself from his own blackness in attempting to identify black women only by their sex.)

The wife has never considered herself a feminist—though she is, of course, a "womanist."* A womanist is a feminist, only more common. (The author of this piece is a womanist.) So she is surprised when her husband attacks her as a "women's libber," a "white women's lackey," a "pawn" in the hands of Gloria Steinem, an incipient bra-burner! What possible connection could there be, he wants to know, between her and white women—those overprivi-ledged hags now (he's recently read in *Newsweek*) marching and preaching their puritanical horseshit up and down Times Square!

(He remembers only the freedom he felt there, not her long standing before the window of the plastic doll shop.) And if she is going to make a lot of new connections with dykes and whites, where will that leave him, the black man, the most brutalized and oppressed human being on the face of the earth? (*Is it because he can now ogle white*

* "Womanist" approximates "black feminist."

women in freedom and she has no similar outlet of expression that he thinks of her as still black and himself as something else? This thought underlines what he is actually saying, and his wife is unaware of it.) Didn't she know it is over these very same white bodies he has been lynched in the past, and is lynched still, by the police and the U.S. prison system, dozens of times a year *even now!?*

The wife has cunningly saved Tracey A. Gardner's essay for just this moment. Because Tracey A. Gardner has thought about it *all*, not just presently, but historically, and she is clear about all the abuse being done to herself as a black person and as a woman, and she is bold and she is cold—she is furious. The wife, given more to depression and self-abnegation than to fury, basks in the fire of Gardner's high-spirited anger.

She begins to read:

> *Because from my point of view, racism is everywhere, including in the women's movement, and the only time I really need to say anything about it is when I do not see it ... and the first time that happens, I will tell you about it.*

The husband, surprised, thinks this very funny, not to say pertinent. He slaps his knee and sits up. He is dying to make some sort of positive dyke comment, but nothing comes to mind.

> *American slavery relied on the denial of the humanity of Black folks, and the undermining of our sense of nationhood and family, on the stripping away of the Black man's role as protector and provider, and on the structuring of Black women into the American system of white male domination....*

"In other words," she says, "white men think they have to be on top. Other men have been known to savor life from other positions."

The end of the Civil War brought the end of a certain "form" of slavery for Black folks. It also brought the end of any "job security" and the loss of the protection of their white enslaver. Blacks were now free game, and the terrorization and humiliation of Black people, especially Black men, began anew. Now the Black man could have his family and prove his worth, but he had no way to support or protect them, or himself. . . .

As she reads, he feels ashamed and senses his wife's wounded embarrassment, for him and for herself. For their history together. But doggedly, she continues to read:

After the Civil War, popular justice, which meant there usually was no trial and no proof needed, began its reign in the form of the castration, burning at the stake, beheading, and lynching of Black men. As many as 5,000 white people would turn out to witness these events, as though going to a celebration. [She pauses, sighs: beheading?] Over 2,000 Black men were lynched in a 10 year period from 1889–99. There were also a number of Black women lynched. [She reads this sentence quickly and forgets it.] Over 50% of the lynched Black males were charged with rape or attempted rape.

He cannot imagine a woman being lynched. He has never even considered the possibility. Perhaps this is why the image of a black woman chained and bruised excites rather than horrifies him? It is the fact that the lynching of her body has never stopped that forces the wife, for the time being, to blot out the historical record. She is not prepared to connect her own husband with the continuation of that past.

She reads:

If a Black man had sex with a consenting white woman, it was rape. [Why am I always reading about, thinking about, worrying about, my man having sex with white women? she thinks, despairingly, underneath the reading.] *If he insulted a white woman by looking at her, it was attempted rape.*

"Yes," he says softly, as if in support of her dogged reading, "I've read Ida B.—what's her last name?"

"By their lynchings, the white man was showing that he hated the Black man carnally, biologically; he hated his color, his features, his genitals. Thus he attacked the Black man's body, and like a lover gone mad, maimed his flesh, violated him in the most intimate, pornographic fashion. . . ."
I believe that this obscene, inhuman treatment of Black men by white men, has a direct correlation to white men's increasingly obscene and inhuman treatment of women, particularly white women, in pornography and real life. White women, working towards their own strength and identity, their own sexuality, have in a sense become uppity niggers. As the Black man threatens the white man's masculinity and power, so now do women.

"That girl's onto something," says the husband, but thinks, for the first time in his life, that when he is not thinking of fucking white women—fantasizing over *Jiveboy* or clucking at them on the street—he is very often thinking of ways to humiliate them. Then he thinks that, given his history as a black man in America, it is not surprising that he has himself confused fucking them *with* humiliating them. But what does that say about how he sees himself? This thought smothers his inward applause for Gardner, and instead he casts a bewildered, disconcerted look at his wife. He knows that to make love to his wife as she really is, as who she really is—indeed, to make love to any other human being as they really are— will require a soul-rending look into himself, and the thought of this virtually straightens his hair.

His wife continues:

Some Black men, full of the white man's perspective and values, see the white woman or Blond Goddess as part of the American winning image. Sometimes when he is with the Black woman, he is ashamed of how she has been treated and how he has been powerless, and that they have always had to work together and protect each other. [Yes, she thinks, we were always all we had, until now. He thinks: We are all we have still, only now we can live without permitting ourselves to know this.] *Frantz Fanon said about white women, "By loving me she proves that I am worthy of white love. I am loved like a white man. I am a white man. I marry the culture, white beauty, white whiteness. When my restless hands caress those white breasts, they grasp white civilization and dignity and make them mine."* [She cannot believe he meant to write "white dignity."]

She pauses, looks at her husband: "So how does a black woman feel when her black man leaves *Playboy* on the coffee table?"

For the first time he understands fully a line his wife read the day before: "The pornography industry's exploitation of the black woman's body is *qualitatively* different from that of the white woman," because she is holding the cover of *Jivers* out to him and asking: "What does this woman look like?"

What he has refused to see—because to see it would reveal yet another area in which he is unable to protect or defend black women—is that where white women are depicted in pornography as "objects," black women are depicted as animals. Where white women are depicted at least as human bodies if not beings, black women are depicted as shit.

He begins to feel sick. For he realizes that he has bought some if not all of the advertisements about women, black and white. And further, inevitably, he has bought the advertisements about himself. In pornography the black man is portrayed as being capable of fucking anything

. . . even a piece of shit. He is defined solely by the size, readiness and unselectivity of his cock.

Still, he does not know how to make love without the fantasies fed to him by movies and magazines. Those movies and magazines (whose characters' pursuits are irrelevant or antithetical to his concerns) that have insinuated themselves between him and his wife, so that the totality of her body, her entire corporeal reality is alien to him. Even to clutch her in lust is automatically to shut his eyes. Shut his eyes, and . . . he chuckles bitterly . . . dream of England.

For years he has been fucking himself.

At first, reading Lorde together, they reject celibacy. Then they discover they need time apart to clear their heads, to search out damage, to heal. In any case, she is unable to fake response; he is unwilling for her to do so. She goes away for a while. Left alone, he soon falls hungrily on the magazines he had thrown out. Strokes himself raw over the beautiful women, spread like so much melon (he begins to see how stereotypes transmute) before him. But he cannot refuse what he knows—or what he knows his wife knows, walking along a beach in some black country where all the women are bleached and straightened and the men never look at themselves; and are ugly, in any case, in their imitation of white men.

Long before she returns he is reading her books and thinking of her—and of her struggles alone and his fear of sharing them—and when she returns, it is sixty percent *her* body that he moves against in the sun, her own black skin affirmed in the brightness of his eyes.

FAME

"In order to *see* anything, and therefore to create," Andrea Clement White was saying to the young woman seated across from her and listening very attentively, "one must not be famous."

"But *you* are famous," said the young woman, in mock perplexity, for the television cameras.

"Am I?" asked Andrea Clement White, and then added, "I suppose I am. But not *really* famous, you know, like . . . like . . ." But she could not bring herself to utter a rival's name, because this would increase the rival's fame, she felt, while diminishing her own.

"Your books have sold millions of copies," the young interviewer was saying. "They've been translated into a dozen languages. Into German and Dutch and Portuguese . . ."

"Into Spanish and French and Japanese and Italian and

Swahili," Andrea Clement White completed the list for her, omitting, because they never came to mind, Russian, Greek, Polish and Lithuanian.

"And you've made from your work, how much? Hundreds of thousands of dollars. Isn't that true?"

"Yes, yes," said Andrea Clement White, in a little girl's voice that mixed pride with peevishness. "I can't complain, as to sales."

And so the interview continued. A gentle interrogation with no embarrassing questions, because Andrea Clement White was now old and had become an institution and there was never anyone in her presence who did not evince respect.

"Let me put it this way," she said. "It is more important that they are *people*, from the novelist's point of view. A botanist might say of a flower, it is a *red* flower. He is really studying flowers."

(Her mind had switched to automatic. No one had asked an interesting question in years.)

If she was famous, she wondered fretfully behind the alert face she raised for television, why didn't she *feel* famous? She had made money, as the young woman— lamentably informed in other respects—had said. Lots of money. Thousands upon thousands of dollars. She had seen her work accepted around the world, welcomed even, which was more than she'd ever dreamed possible for it. And yet—there remained an emptiness, no, an ache, which told her she had not achieved what she had set out to achieve. And instead must live out her life always in the shadow of those who had accomplished more than she, or had, in any case, received a wider and more fervid recognition. But, on closer scrutiny, those "others" she immediately thought of—the talk show guests, the much reviewed, the oft quoted—had *not* received more acclaim or been more praised than she; why then did she feel they had?

(She knew she would not be satisfied with the interview

when it was aired. She would come across as a fatuous, smug know-everything, or as an irritable, spacy old fool. Her chronic dissatisfaction was always captured by television, no matter how cleverly she tried to disguise it as, oh, fatigue, too much to think about, doddering old age, or whatever.)

She left the studio thinking of the luncheon for her that same afternoon. It was at the college where she'd taught English literature (how she'd *struggled* to prove Charles Chesnutt wrote in English!) for over a decade. The president would be there and all her colleagues, with whom she'd battled, sometimes successfully, sometimes not (for five years they'd resisted Chesnutt, for example) over the years. They would fulsomely praise her—obliterating from memory the times they'd wished her dead; she would graciously acquiesce. She thought of Cooke, the dean, now retired of course, but unthinkable that he would not show up; how he had always been the first to kiss her whenever she returned from even the slightest triumph, and how she had detested that kiss—his lips rough, cluttered and gluey —and how she had told him, explicitly, her feelings. "But ladies are *meant* to be kissed!" he replied. She had thrown up her hands—and endured. Or had avoided him, which, because they shared an office, was not easy.

Then there was Mrs. Hyde, her secretary, also retired from the college though still working for Andrea Clement White in her office at home, who was the closest thing she had to someone to lean on. Any time of the day or night she was able to call on Mrs. Hyde—and Mrs. Hyde seemed to have nothing better to do than serve her. She understood she represented to Mrs. Hyde a glamour utterly missing from her own life, and Andrea Clement White had, over the thirty years of *their* acquaintanceship, ridiculed *Mr.* Hyde unmercifully. Because, in truth, she grew used to being served by Mrs. Hyde, had come to expect her service as her due, and was jealous and contemptuous of

Mr. Hyde—a dull little man with the flat, sour cheeks of a snake—who provided his wife little of the excitement Andrea Clement White felt was generated spontaneously in her own atmosphere.

Mrs. Hyde was, in fact, driving the car, Mrs. Clement White seated beside her. And one could tell from the restful silence in the car that they shared a very real life together. If Andrea Clement White sat in the same car with her husband it was clear *they* shared a life. He was a man who cared little for Literature, having—as he said—married it and seen how crazy it was. But the quality of the silence was quite different. In her husband's silence there was tension, criticism of her, impatience. He held his tongue the better to make her know what he thought. Mrs. Hyde held hers as a comfort; she knew Mrs. Clement White needed the silence—after an encounter with other people—to settle into herself again.

"Imagine thinking that black people write only about being black and not about being people." Andrea Clement White fumed, rummaging through her purse for a tissue. "Disgusting make-up," she said, running a tissue around her collar and bringing it down a very dark brown. "Can you imagine, as many shades of brown as there are, they have only one jar to cover everything? And one jar, of course, for *them*, but then *they* only need one jar." Mrs. Hyde did not say anything. She drove expertly, smoothly. Enjoying the luxury of the car, a silver Mercedes 350SL. Her foot barely touched the pedal and the car *slid* along, effortlessly.

I walked into the studio, Andrea Clement White replayed herself, as she did all the time (someone called this the curse—or was it the blessing?—of the artist; she thought everyone did it), and right away, as usual, I knew it was going to be awful. That the questions would be boring and the interviewer ill read, ahistorical and poorly educated. It was enough when white liberals told you they considered what you said or wrote to be new in the world (and one was expected to fall for this flattery); one never expected them to know one's history well enough to recognize an evolution, a variation, when they saw it; they meant *new* to *them*. But how cutely ignorant the young black woman interviewer had been! "You are the first!" she had boomed—strangely unbleached black voice as yet, but TV would whiten it out—and when Andrea Clement White said, "But there's no such thing as a first, an absolute first in the area of human relations, only perhaps in Science," the woman had thought her coy, and had grinned, indulgently. (Andrea Clement White hated to be indulged when she was not seeking indulgence. It was at that point that she switched her mind to automatic.)

And now the lilacs along the road rushed as if drawn against the silver of the car; and lilacs and television interviewer mixed: there was an image of the interviewer with a sprig of lilacs in her hair. But why so many so far south? Had they been creeping south with the harsher winters? Or had they been here always? Andrea Clement White could not remember. She saw herself among the lilacs on her college campus in upstate New York. I stood *drenched* in the smell of lilacs. It was my perfume for twenty years, with one year out for an experiment with patchouli. . . .

Mrs. Hyde had stopped the car and reached into the back seat and fetched up the cane that made walking a somewhat more steady affair for Mrs. Clement White. It was a lovely oak cane, hand carved by a famous eighteenth-century carver who fell into the hands of a mistress who demanded twenty such carved canes a week; these she sold in the marketplace in Charleston, and thus, after her husband lost his money gambling and ran off with a woman who supplied him with more, she had supported herself. The carver, sick of carving and unbelieving that the Civil War would free the slaves, and too much of a gentleman to rebel or run away from a helpless white woman who

58

needed him, cut off three fingers from his left hand, "accidentally," while "branching" a tree. But he had not reckoned on the Scarlett O'Hara persistence of his mistress. She limited the number of canes she expected weekly to fifteen.

I was standing watching Ben make the canes, thought Andrea Clement White, because I was his daughter. Was I pretty? She thought probably she was. And she had been his other hand until freedom came. Freedom had come and everyone had had ideas about what it was for, even Ben. He had simply died. I was at the burying, of course. It was I, in fact, who dug the grave, along with . . . then she wondered if she would have had to be a boy to help dig the grave. She saw herself as one. Handsome, was he? She thought probably yes. But then she thought she would not have had to be a boy to do it because she had been doing every kind of work on the plantation *as a girl,* and no one thought anything of it, so she'd stay a girl. She sighed with relief.

Rudolph Miller opened the car door on her side and she looked out and up into his lapel. He had the unctuous, shit-eating grin she'd despised for—thirty years. How had she stood it without throwing up? It seemed to be made of wet papier-mâché. Took his hand: dry, plump, *old* hand, horny nails. *Yuck.* (Her grandchildren's expressions came in handy at times like this.) Mrs. Hyde trotted around the car with the cane. So fat, Mrs. Hyde, and given to hyperventilation. But oh, the lilacs! Even here. "When lilacs last in the dooryard bloomed . . ." Abe Lincoln had probably never dreamed there would be colleges like this, for blacks, in the South. What *had* he dreamed? To be better looking, she didn't doubt.

Now she had liver spots on her cheeks and her hair was slowly receding, but that wasn't so bad. She could look infinitely worse and there'd still be a luncheon for her, a banquet later tonight and book parties and telegrams and people *beaming* at her well into the future. Success was the best bone structure. Or the best cosmetic. But was she a success? she asked herself. And herself answered, in a chorus, *exasperated*, Of *Course* You Are! Only a small voice near the back faltered. She stifled it.

There was, oh, McGeorge Grundy. Bundy. Ford Foundation. Going up the stairs. (They had really scrounged for dignitaries for this affair.) It would turn into a fund raiser, as everything did. And did she mind? She was making a speech as McGeorge: I give you all the money in one lump. You'll never have to worry about money again. Or beg. Period. Good-bye. Cheering. Throwing of hats in the air. People actually used to do that. But few people wore hats today. Of course Nigerians, she heard, threw people, but that was depressing.

"This little lady has done . . ." Would he have said "This little man . . ."? But of course not. No man wanted to be called little. He thought it referred to his penis. But to say "little lady" made men think of virgins. Tight, tiny pussies, and moments of rape.

But this was fame, thought Andrea Clement White, poking at her Rock Cornish hen, which slid gracefully if speedily into Mrs. Hyde's lap. There are the multitudes. *Is* the multitude? Anyhow, every bored, numbskull student I ever taught, every mediocre professor I've ever wanted to axe. And the president doing what he does best—"This little lady" . . .

It was probably with the patchouli that she had caught William Litz White, her husband. He'd never smelled anything like it—successful doctor, intense billiards player that he was—and had never intended to. Bohemian. Bohemian Belle, he had called her. She had wanted to *be* bohemian: to write on a kitchen table perhaps; but *not* among her children's unwashed cereal bowls. Patchouli was as close as she got.

The hen was still nesting on Mrs. Hyde's lap. Like most people who are not famous a small thing like getting a Rock Cornish hen out of her lap and back on the table paralyzed her. How could she be so indecorous as to plop the bird back into Andrea Clement White's plate? That famous and fastidious lady (she had read interviews to the effect that she *was* fastidious; this was not necessarily her own opinion). She began to sweat.

"He's a bore," said Andrea Clement White, audibly and viciously (she had discovered viciousness amused)—but then, she was forgiven everything because of her fame, her use as a fund raiser, and age—and began to feel around Mrs. Hyde's broad knees for the tiny chicken. Dragging it up stuck to Mrs. Hyde's dress—Mrs. Hyde meanwhile going gray with embarrassment—Mrs. Clement White raised it to her lips—and took a bite.

Five hundred in the audience did the same.

Was there a point, she wondered, chewing, in thinking about what one ate at functions like this? The rocklike hen, the red ring of spicy, soggy apple. The broccoli that no one in the South had learned to cook, only to boil? She thought not, and ate it all without thinking beyond the fact that she was hungry, had to pee, was bored to tears, and her bra strap was biting into the radical edges of her latest mastectomy.

A slow, aged string of tipsy wasps (he who owned the newspaper that said Negroes had no use for higher education, though perhaps the trades; she who told far and wide the remarkable insights of her grandmother's enslaved cook; he who . . .) now rose to drone her praises. She munched her chicken and five hundred others munched along with her, their chewing a noisy, incessant and exhuberant ignoring. She was suddenly back at the plantation. But where? Mississippi? Too hot, and already a cliché. Ditto Alabama, Georgia and Louisiana. She picked Virginia, where there were cool mountains and where it was not too severe a stretch of the imagination to match five hundred and one chickens to that many hungry slaves. *Crunch.* She was smiling and chewing but without any intention of listening. She nodded—still grinning and chewing as each person sat down. "In *spite* of you I'm sitting here," she thought, and reached over for the apple ring from Mrs. Hyde's plate. This second apple ring was always saved for her to eat at the end of the meal. It was her mouthwash.

She projected herself ahead a few minutes to being presented to the audience by Tedious Taylor, the president: she was battling him with her eyes. DON'T YOU *DARE* KISS ME! But he closed his froglike eyes, descended his head, his pendulous lips, and kissed the most prominent of her liver spots. *Yuck.* So *many* Yucks. Because then there would creep up behind her Dean Cooke (whom she would have kept tabs on until now), who would glue his mouth to her neck in an attitude of falling.

She saw herself hit him in the groin with her award, a sharp-beaked silver goose. But was it a silver goose? It would be duck, swan or goose. (Bird awards were lately "in.") Perhaps all three, and it would be not silver but silver plate, and there would be eggs. (She was a woman, after all!) Golden.

She felt briefly terrific, imagining Cooke's piglike squeal, and gnawed her chicken savagely, her eyes quite glazed over, in abstracted glee.

But now there came in front of the audience—with a slight bow to Mrs. Clement White—a small girl the color of chocolate. But *really* the color of chocolate. Hack writers always said black people were chocolate colored; this saved them the work of looking. Andrea Clement White was amused that this child really was the exact shade of brown of a chocolate drop.

She opened her mouth and began to sing with assurance an old, emphatically familiar song.

A slave song. Authorless.

Picked drumsticks fell onto plates like hail. Profound silence at last prevailed.

And it was this child's confident memory, *that* old anonymous song, that gave Andrea Clement White the energy to stand up and endure with dignity (the audience surreptitiously nibbling at dessert as she began to speak) the presentation of her one hundred and eleventh major award.

THE
ABORTION

They had discussed it, but not deeply, whether they wanted the baby she was now carrying. "I don't *know* if I want it," she said, eyes filling with tears. She cried at anything now, and was often nauseous. That pregnant women cried easily and were nauseous seemed banal to her, and she resented banality.

"Well, think about it," he said, with his smooth reassuring voice (but with an edge of impatience she now felt) that used to soothe her.

It was all she *did* think about, all she apparently *could*; that he could dream otherwise enraged her. But she always lost, when they argued. Her temper would flare up, he would become instantly reasonable, mature, responsible, if not responsive precisely, to her mood, and she would swallow down her tears and hate herself. It was because she believed him "good." The best human being she had ever met.

"It isn't as if we don't already have a child," she said in a calmer tone, carelessly wiping at the tear that slid from one eye.

"We have a perfect child," he said with relish, "thank the Good Lord!"

Had she ever dreamed she'd marry someone humble enough to go around thanking the Good Lord? She had not.

Now they left the bedroom, where she had been lying down on their massive king-size bed with the forbidding ridge in the middle, and went down the hall—hung with bright prints—to the cheerful, spotlessly clean kitchen. He put water on for tea in a bright yellow pot.

She wanted him to want the baby so much he would try to save its life. On the other hand, she did not permit such presumptuousness. As he praised the child they already had, a daughter of sunny disposition and winning smile, Imani sensed subterfuge, and hardened her heart.

"What am I talking about," she said, as if she'd been talking about it. "Another child would kill me. I can't imagine life with two children. Having a child is a good experience *to have had*, like graduate school. But if you've had one, you've had the experience and that's enough."

He placed the tea before her and rested a heavy hand on her hair. She felt the heat and pressure of his hand as she touched the cup and felt the odor and steam rise up from it. Her throat contracted.

"I can't drink that," she said through gritted teeth. "Take it away."

There were days of this.

Clarice, their daughter, was barely two years old. A miscarriage brought on by grief (Imani had lost her fervidly

environmentalist mother to lung cancer shortly after
Clarice's birth; the asbestos ceiling in the classroom where
she taught first graders had leaked for twenty years) separated Clarice's birth from the new pregnancy. Imani felt
her body had been assaulted by these events and was, in
fact, considerably weakened, and was also, in any case,
chronically anaemic and run down. Still, if she had wanted
the baby more than she did not want it, she would not
have planned to abort it.

They lived in a small town in the South. Her husband,
Clarence, was, among other things, legal adviser and de-
fender of the new black mayor of the town. The mayor
was much in their lives because of the difficulties being the
first black mayor of a small town assured, and because,
next to the major leaders of black struggles in the South,
Clarence respected and admired him most.

Imani reserved absolute judgment, but she did point
out that Mayor Carswell would never look at her directly
when she made a comment or posed a question, even sitting at her own dinner table, and would instead talk to
Clarence as if she were not there. He assumed that as a
woman she would not be interested in, or even understand,
politics. (He would comment occasionally on her cooking
or her clothes. He noticed when she cut her hair.) But
Imani understood every shade and variation of politics:
she understood, for example, why she fed the mouth that
did not speak to her; because for the present she must
believe in Mayor Carswell, even as he could not believe in
her. Even understanding this, however, she found dinners
with Carswell hard to swallow.

But Clarence was dedicated to the mayor, and believed
his success would ultimately mean security and advance-
ment for them all.

On the morning she left to have the abortion, the mayor
and Clarence were to have a working lunch, and they drove
her to the airport deep in conversation about municipal

funds, racist cops, and the facilities for teaching at the chaotic, newly integrated schools. Clarence had time for the briefest kiss and hug at the airport ramp.

"Take care of yourself," he whispered lovingly as she walked away. He was needed, while she was gone, to draft the city's new charter. She had agreed this was important; the mayor was already being called incompetent by local businessmen and the chamber of commerce, and one inferred from television that no black person alive even knew what a city charter was.

"Take care of myself." Yes, she thought. I see that is what I have to do. But she thought this self-pityingly, which invalidated it. She had expected *him* to take care of her, and she blamed him for not doing so now.

Well, she was a fraud, anyway. She had known after a year of marriage that it bored her. "The Experience of Having a Child" was to distract her from this fact. Still, she expected him to "take care of her." She was lucky he didn't pack up and leave. But he seemed to know, as she did, that if anyone packed and left, it would be her. Precisely *because* she was a fraud and because in the end he would settle for fraud and she could not.

On the plane to New York her teeth ached and she vomited bile—bitter, yellowish stuff she hadn't even been aware her body produced. She resented and appreciated the crisp help of the stewardess, who asked if she needed anything, then stood chatting with the cigarette-smoking white man next to her, whose fat hairy wrist, like a large worm, was all Imani could bear to see out of the corner of her eye.

Her first abortion, when she was still in college, she frequently remembered as wonderful, bearing as it had all the marks of a supreme coming of age and a seizing of the direction of her own life, as well as a comprehension of existence that never left her: that life—what one saw about one and called Life—was not a facade. There was nothing

behind it which used "Life" as its manifestation. Life was
itself. Period. At the time, and afterwards, and even now,
this seemed a marvelous thing to know.

The abortionist had been a delightful Italian doctor on
the Upper East Side in New York, and before he put her
under he told her about his own daughter who was just her
age, and a junior at Vassar. He babbled on and on until
she was out, but not before Imani had thought how her
thousand dollars, for which she would be in debt for years,
would go to keep her there.

When she woke up it was all over. She lay on a brown
Naugahyde sofa in the doctor's outer office. And she heard,
over her somewhere in the air, the sound of a woman's
voice. It was a Saturday, no nurses in attendance, and she
presumed it was the doctor's wife. She was pulled gently
to her feet by this voice and encouraged to walk.

"And when you leave, be sure to walk as if nothing is
wrong," the voice said.

Imani did not feel any pain. This surprised her. Perhaps
he didn't do anything, she thought. Perhaps he took my
thousand dollars and put me to sleep with two dollars'
worth of ether. Perhaps this is a racket.

But he was so kind, and he was smiling benignly, almost
fatherly, at her (and Imani realized how desperately she
needed this "fatherly" look, this "fatherly" smile). "Thank
you," she murmured sincerely: she was thanking him for
her life.

Some of Italy was still in his voice. "It's nothing, nothing," he said. "A nice, pretty girl like you; in school like
my own daughter, you didn't need this trouble."

"He's nice," she said to herself, walking to the subway
on her way back to school. She lay down gingerly across a
vacant seat, and passed out.

She hemorrhaged steadily for six weeks, and was not
well again for a year.

*   *   *

But this was seven years later. An abortion law now made it possible to make an appointment at a clinic, and for seventy-five dollars a safe, quick, painless abortion was yours.

Imani had once lived in New York, in the Village, not five blocks from where the abortion clinic was. It was also near the Margaret Sanger clinic, where she had received her very first diaphragm, with utter gratitude and amazement that someone apparently understood and actually cared about young women as alone and ignorant as she. In fact, as she walked up the block, with its modern office buildings side by side with older, more elegant brownstones, she felt how close she was still to that earlier self. Still not in control of her sensuality, and only through violence and with money (for the flight, for the operation itself) in control of her body.

She found that abortion had entered the age of the assembly line. Grateful for the lack of distinction between herself and the other women—all colors, ages, states of misery or nervousness—she was less happy to notice, once the doctor started to insert the catheter, that the anesthesia she had been given was insufficient. But assembly lines don't stop because the product on them has a complaint. Her doctor whistled, and assured her she was all right, and carried the procedure through to the horrific end. Imani fainted some seconds before that.

They laid her out in a peaceful room full of cheerful colors. Primary colors: yellow, red, blue. When she revived she had the feeling of being in a nursery. She had a pressing need to urinate.

A nurse, kindly, white-haired and with firm hands, helped her to the toilet. Imani saw herself in the mirror over the sink and was alarmed. She was literally gray, as if all her blood had leaked out.

"Don't worry about how you look," said the nurse.

"Rest a bit here and take it easy when you get back home. You'll be fine in a week or so."

She could not imagine being fine again. Somewhere her child—she never dodged into the language of "fetuses" and "amorphous growths"—was being flushed down a sewer. Gone all her or his chances to see the sunlight, savor a fig.

"Well," she said to this child, "it was you or me, Kiddo, and I chose me."

There were people who thought she had no right to choose herself, but Imani knew better than to think of those people now.

It was a bright, hot Saturday when she returned.

Clarence and Clarice picked her up at the airport. They had brought flowers from Imani's garden, and Clarice presented them with a stout-hearted hug. Once in her mother's lap she rested content all the way home, sucking her thumb, stroking her nose with the forefinger of the same hand, and kneading a corner of her blanket with the three fingers that were left.

"How did it go?" asked Clarence.

"It went," said Imani.

There was no way to explain abortion to a man. She thought castration might be an apt analogy, but most men, perhaps all, would insist this could not possibly be true.

"The anesthesia failed," she said. "I thought I'd never faint in time to keep from screaming and leaping off the table."

Clarence paled. He hated the thought of pain, any kind of violence. He could not endure it; it made him physically ill. This was one of the reasons he was a pacifist, another reason she admired him.

She knew he wanted her to stop talking. But she continued in a flat, deliberate voice.

"All the blood seemed to run out of me. The tendons in my legs felt cut. I was gray."

He reached for her hand. Held it. Squeezed.

"But," she said, "at least I know what I don't want. And I intend never to go through any of this again."

They were in the living room of their peaceful, quiet and colorful house. Imani was in her rocker, Clarice dozing on her lap. Clarence sank to the floor and rested his head against her knees. She felt he was asking for nurture when she needed it herself. She felt the two of them, Clarence and Clarice, clinging to her, using her. And that the only way she could claim herself, feel herself distinct from them, was by doing something painful, self-defining but self-destructive.

She suffered the pressure of his head as long as she could.

"Have a vasectomy," she said, "or stay in the guest room. Nothing is going to touch me anymore that isn't harmless."

He smoothed her thick hair with his hand. "We'll talk about it," he said, as if that was not what they were doing. "We'll see. Don't worry. We'll take care of things."

She had forgotten that the third Sunday in June, the following day, was the fifth memorial observance for Holly Monroe, who had been shot down on her way home from her high-school graduation ceremony five years before. Imani *always* went to these memorials. She liked the reassurance that her people had long memories, and that those people who fell in struggle or innocence were not forgotten. She was, of course, too weak to go. She was dizzy and still losing blood. The white lawgivers attempted to get around assassination—which Imani considered extreme abortion—by saying the victim provoked it (there had been some difficulty saying this about Holly Monroe, but they had tried) but were antiabortionist to a man. Imani thought of this as she resolutely showered and washed her hair.

Clarence had installed central air conditioning their second year in the house. Imani had at first objected. "I want to smell the trees, the flowers, the natural air!" she cried. But the first summer of 110-degree heat had cured her of giving a damn about any of that. Now she wanted to be cool. As much as she loved trees, on a hot day she would have sawed through a forest to get to an air conditioner.

In fairness to him, she had to admit he asked her if she thought she was well enough to go. But even to be asked annoyed her. She was not one to let her own troubles prevent her from showing proper respect and remembrance toward the dead, although she understood perfectly well that once dead, the dead do not exist. So respect, remembrance was for herself, and today herself needed rest. There was something mad about her refusal to rest, and she felt it as she tottered about getting Clarice dressed. But she did not stop. She ran a bath, plopped the child in it, scrubbed her plump body on her knees, arms straining over the tub awkwardly in a way that made her stomach hurt—but not yet her uterus—dried her hair, lifted her out and dried the rest of her on the kitchen table.

"You are going to remember as long as you live what kind of people they are," she said to the child, who, gurgling and cooing, looked into her mother's stern face with light-hearted fixation.

"You are going to hear the music," Imani said. "The music they've tried to kill. The music they try to steal." She felt feverish and was aware she was muttering. She didn't care.

"They think they can kill a continent—people, trees, buffalo—and then fly off to the moon and just forget about it. But you and me we're going to remember the people, the trees and the fucking buffalo. Goddammit."

"Buffwoe," said the child, hitting at her mother's face with a spoon.

She placed the baby on a blanket in the living room and turned to see her husband's eyes, full of pity, on her. She wore pert green velvet slippers and a lovely sea green robe. Her body was bent within it. A reluctant tear formed beneath his gaze.

"Sometimes I look at you and I wonder 'What is this man doing in my house?' "

This had started as a joke between them. Her aim had been never to marry, but to take in lovers who could be sent home at dawn, freeing her to work and ramble.

"I'm here because you love me," was the traditional answer. But Clarence faltered, meeting her eyes, and Imani turned away.

It was a hundred degrees by ten o'clock. By eleven, when the memorial service began, it would be ten degrees hotter. Imani staggered from the heat. When she sat in the car she had to clench her teeth against the dizziness until the motor prodded the air conditioning to envelop them in coolness. A dull ache started in her uterus.

The church was not of course air conditioned. It was authentic Primitive Baptist in every sense.

Like the four previous memorials this one was designed by Holly Monroe's classmates. All twenty-five of whom— fat and thin—managed to look like the dead girl. Imani had never seen Holly Monroe, though there were always photographs of her dominating the pulpit of this church where she had been baptized and where she had sung in the choir—and to her, every black girl of a certain vulnerable age *was* Holly Monroe. And an even deeper truth was that Holly Monroe was herself. Herself shot down, aborted on the eve of becoming herself.

She was prepared to cry and to do so with abandon. But she did not. She clenched her teeth against the steadily increasing pain and her tears were instantly blotted by the heat.

Mayor Carswell had been waiting for Clarence in the

vestibule of the church, mopping his plumply jowled face with a voluminous handkerchief and holding court among half a dozen young men and women who listened to him with awe. Imani exchanged greetings with the mayor, he ritualistically kissed her on the cheek, and kissed Clarice on the cheek, but his rather heat-glazed eye was already fastened on her husband. The two men huddled in a corner away from the awed young group. Away from Imani and Clarice, who passed hesitantly, waiting to be joined or to be called back, into the church.

There was a quarter hour's worth of music.

"Holly Monroe was five feet, three inches tall, and weighed one hundred and eleven pounds," her best friend said, not reading from notes, but talking to each person in the audience. "She was a stubborn, loyal Aries, the best kind of friend to have. She had black kinky hair that she experimented with a lot. She was exactly the color of this oak church pew in the summer; in the winter she was the color [pointing up] of this heart pine ceiling. She loved green. She did not like lavender because she said she also didn't like pink. She had brown eyes and wore glasses, except when she was meeting someone for the first time. She had a sort of rounded nose. She had beautiful large teeth, but her lips were always chapped so she didn't smile as much as she might have if she'd ever gotten used to carrying Chap Stick. She had elegant feet.

"Her favorite church song was 'Leaning on the Everlasting Arms.' Her favorite other kind of song was 'I Can't Help Myself—I Love You and Nobody Else.' She was often late for choir rehearsal though she loved to sing. She made the dress she wore to her graduation in Home Ec. She *hated* Home Ec. . . ."

Imani was aware that the sound of low, murmurous voices had been the background for this statement all along. Everything was quiet around her, even Clarice sat up straight, absorbed by the simple friendliness of the young woman's voice. All of Holly Monroe's classmates and friends in the choir wore vivid green. Imani imagined Clarice entranced by the brilliant, swaying color as by a field of swaying corn.

Lifting the child, her uterus burning, and perspiration already a stream down her back, Imani tiptoed to the door. Clarence and the mayor were still deep in conversation. She heard "board meeting . . . aldermen . . . city council." She beckoned to Clarence.

"Your voices are carrying!" she hissed.

She meant: How dare you not come inside.

They did not. Clarence raised his head, looked at her, and shrugged his shoulders helplessly. Then, turning, with the abstracted air of priests, the two men moved slowly toward the outer door, and into the churchyard, coming to stand some distance from the church beneath a large oak tree. There they remained throughout the service.

Two years later, Clarence was furious with her: What is the matter with you? he asked. You never want me to touch you. You told me to sleep in the guest room and I did. You told me to have a vasectomy I didn't want and *I did.* (Here, there was a sob of hatred for her somewhere in the anger, the humiliation: he thought of himself as a eunuch, and blamed her.)

She was not merely frigid, she was remote.

She had been amazed after they left the church that the anger she'd felt watching Clarence and the mayor turn away from the Holly Monroe memorial did not prevent her accepting a ride home with him. A month later it did not prevent her smiling on him fondly. Did not prevent a trip to Bermuda, a few blissful days of very good sex on a deserted beach screened by trees. Did not prevent her listening to his mother's stories of Clarence's youth as though she would treasure them forever.

And yet. From that moment in the heat at the church

door, she had uncoupled herself from him, in a separation that made him, except occasionally, little more than a stranger.

And he had not felt it, had not known.

"What have I done?" he asked, all the tenderness in his voice breaking over her. She smiled a nervous smile at him, which he interpreted as derision—so far apart had they drifted.

They had discussed the episode at the church many times. Mayor Carswell—whom they never saw anymore—was now a model mayor, with wide biracial support in his campaign for the legislature. Neither could easily recall him, though television frequently brought him into the house.

"It was so important that I help the mayor!" said Clarence. "He was our *first!*"

Imani understood this perfectly well, but it sounded humorous to her. When she smiled, he was offended.

She had known the moment she left the marriage, the exact second. But apparently that moment had left no perceptible mark.

They argued, she smiled, they scowled, blamed and cried—as she packed.

Each of them almost recalled out loud that about this time of the year their aborted child would have been a troublesome, "terrible" two-year-old, a great burden on its mother, whose health was by now in excellent shape, each wanted to think aloud that the marriage would have deteriorated anyway, because of that.

PORN

Like many thoughtful women of the seventies, she had
decided women were far more interesting than men. But,
again like most thoughtful women, she rarely admitted
this aloud. Besides, again like her contemporaries, she
maintained a close connection with a man.

It was a sexual connection.

They had met in Tanzania when it was still Tanganyika;
she was with an international group of students interested
in health care in socialist African countries; he with an
American group intent upon building schools. They met.
Liked each other. Wrote five or six letters over the next
seven years. Married other people. Had children. Lived in
different cities. Divorced. Met again to discover they now
shared a city and lived barely three miles apart.

A strong bond between them was that they respected
their former spouses and supported their children. They

had each arranged a joint custody settlement and many of their favorite outings were amid a clash of children. Still, her primary interest in him was sexual. It was not that she did not respect his mind; she did. It was a fine mind. More scientific than hers, more given to abstractions. But also a mind curious about nature and the hidden workings of things (it was probably this, she thought, that made him such a good lover) and she enjoyed following his thoughts about the distances of stars and whole galaxies from the earth, the difference between low clouds and high fog, and the complex survival mechanisms of the snail.

But sex together was incredibly good: like conversation with her women friends, who were never abstract, rarely distant enough from nature to be critical in their appraisal of it, and whose own mechanisms for survival were hauled out in discussion for all to see. The touch of his fingers— sensitive, wise, exploring the furthest reaches of sensation —were like the tongues of women, talking, questing, searching for the *true* place, the place which, when touched, has no choice but to respond.

She was aflame with desire for him.

On those evenings when all the children were with their other parents, he would arrive at the apartment at seven. They would walk hand in hand to a Chinese restaurant a mile away. They would laugh and drink and eat and touch hands and knees over and under the table. They would come home. Smoke a joint. He would put music on. She would run water in the tub with lots of bubbles. In the bath they would lick and suck each other, in blissful delight. They would admire the rich candle glow on their wet, delectably earth-toned skins. Sniff the incense—the odor of sandal and redwood. He would carry her in to bed.

Music. Emotion. Sensation. Presence.
Satisfaction like rivers
flowing and silver.

On the basis of their sexual passion they built the friendship that sustained them through the outings with their collective children, through his loss of a job (temporarily), through her writer's block (she worked as a free-lance journalist), through her bouts of frustration and boredom when she perceived that, in conversation, he could only *be* scientific, only *be* abstract, and she was, because of her intrepid, garrulous women friends—whom she continued frequently, and often in desperation, to see —used to so much more.

In short, they had devised an almost perfect arrangement.

One morning at six o'clock they were making "morning love." "Morning love" was relaxed, clearheaded. Fresh. No music but the birds and cars starting. No dope.

They came within seconds of each other.

This inspired him. He thought they could come together.

She was sated, indifferent, didn't wish to think about the strain.

But then he said: "Did I ever show you [he knew he hadn't] my porn collection?"

"What could it be?" she inevitably wondered. Hooked.

His hands are cupping her ass. His fingers like warm grass or warm and supple vines. One thumb—she fancies she feels the whorled print—makes a circle in the wetness of her anus. She shivers. His tongue gently laps her vulva as it enters her, his top lip caressing the clitoris. For five minutes she is moving along as usual. Blissed *out*, she thinks to herself. Then she stops.

"What have you got?" she has asked him.

"This," he replied. "And this."

* * *

A gorgeous black woman who looks like her friend Fannie has a good friend (white boy from her hometown down South) who is basically gay. Though——. "Fannie" and let us call him "Fred" pick up a hick tourist in a bar. They both dig him, the caption says. He is not gorgeous. He is short, pasty, dirty blond. Slightly cross-eyed. In fact, looks retarded. Fred looks very much the same. "Fannie" invites them to her place where without holding hands or eating or bathing or putting on music, they strip and begin to fondle each other. "Fannie" looks amused as they take turns licking and sucking her. She smiles benignly as they do the same things to each other....

"And this."

A young blonde girl from Minnesota [probably kidnapped, she thinks, reading] *is far from home in New York, lonely and very horny. She is befriended by two of the blackest men on the East Coast. (They had been fighting outside a bar and she had stopped them by flinging her naive white self into the fray.) In their gratitude for her peacemaking they take her to their place and do everything they can think of to her. She grinning liberally the whole time. Finally they make a sandwich of her: one filling the anus and the other the vagina, so that all that is visible of her body between them is a sliver of white thighs.* [And we see that these two pugilists have finally come together on something.]

She is sitting with her back against the headboard of the bed so that her breasts hang down. This increases sensation in her already very aroused nipples. He crawls up to her on all fours like a gentle but ravenous bear and begins to nuzzle her. He nuzzles and nuzzles until her nipples virtually aim themselves at him. He takes one into his mouth. She begins to flow.

But the flow stops.

Once he said to her: "I could be turned on by bondage."
No, he said "by 'a little *light* bondage.'" She had told
him of a fantasy in which she lay helpless, bound, waiting
for the pleasure worse than death.

*There is no plot this time. No story of an improbable
friendship down South, no goldilocks from the Midwestern
plains. Just page after page of women: yellow, red, white,
brown, black* [she had let him tie her up very loosely once;
it was not like her fantasy at all. She had wanted to hold
him, caress him, snuggle and cuddle] *bound, often gagged.
Their legs open. Forced to their knees.*

He is massaging the back of her neck, her shoulders. Her
buttocks. The backs of her thighs. She has bent over a hot
typewriter all day and is tired. She sinks into the feeling
of being desired and pampered. Valued. Loved. Soon she
is completely restored. Alert. She decides to make love to
him. She turns over. She cradles his head in her arms.
Kisses his forehead. His eyes. Massages his scalp with her
fingers. Buries her nose in his neck. Kisses his neck.
Caresses his chest. Flicks his nipples, back and forth, with
her tongue. Slowly she moves down his body. His penis
(which he thinks should not be called "penis"—"a white
boy's word"; he prefers "cock") is standing. She takes it—
she is on her knees—into her mouth.

She gags.

The long-term accommodation that protects marriage and
other such relationships is, she knows, forgetfulness. She
will forget what turns him on.

"No, no," he says, very sorry he has shown her his
collection; in fact, vowing passionately to throw it away.
"The point is for *you* to be turned on by it *too!*"

* * *

She thinks of the lovely black girl—whom she actually thinks of as her friend Fannie—and is horrified. What is Fannie doing in such company? she wonders. She panics as he is entering her. Wait! she says, and races to the phone.

The phone rings and rings.

Her friend Fannie is an out-of-work saleswoman. She is also a lesbian. She proceeds to write in her head a real story about Fannie based on what she knows. Her lover at work on her body the whole time.

Fannie and Laura share a tiny loft apartment. They almost never make love. Not because they are not loving—they do a lot of caressing and soothing—but they are so guilty about what they feel that sexuality has more or less dried up. [She feels her own juices drying up at this thought.]

They have both been out of work for a long time. Laura's mother is sick. Fannie's young brother has entered Howard University. There is only Fannie to send him money for books, clothes and entertainment. Fannie is very pretty but basically unskilled in anything but selling, and salespersons by the thousands have been laid off in the recession. Unemployment is not enough.

But Fannie is really very beautiful. Men stop her on the street all the time to tell her so. It is the way they chose to tell her so, when she was barely pubescent, that makes her return curses for "compliments" even today.

But these men would still stop her on the street, offer her money "for a few hours' work." . . .

By now she has faked all kinds of things, and exhausted her lover. He is sound asleep. She races to Fannie and Laura's apartment. Sits waiting for them on the stoop. Finally they come home from seeing a Woody Allen movie. They are in high spirits, and besides, because she shares part of her life with a man, care much less for her than she does for them. They yawn loudly, kiss her matronizingly on both cheeks, and send her home again.

Now, when he makes love to her, she tries to fit herself into the white-woman, two-black-men story. But who will she be? The men look like her brothers, Bobo and Charlie. She is disgusted, and worse, bored, by Bobo and Charlie. The white woman is like the young girl who, according to the *Times, was* seduced off a farm in Minnesota by a black pimp and turned out on 42nd Street. She cannot stop herself from thinking: *Poor: Ignorant: Sleazy: Depressing.* This does not excite or stimulate.

He watches her face as he makes expert love to her. He knows his technique is virtually flawless, but he thinks perhaps it can be improved. Is she moving less rhythmically under him? Does she seem distracted? There seems to be a separate activity in her body, to which she is attentive, and which is not connected to the current he is sending through his fingertips. He notices the fluttering at the corners of her eyelids. Her eyes could fly open at any moment, he thinks, and look objectively at him. He shudders. Holds her tight.

He thinks frantically of what she might be thinking of him. Realizes he is moving in her *desperately,* as if he is climbing the walls of a closed building. As if she reads his mind, she moans encouragingly. But it is a distracted moan—that offends him.

He bites the pillow over her head: Where *is* she? he thinks. Is she into fantasy or not?

He must be.

He slips her into the role of "Fannie" with some hope. But nothing develops. As "Fannie" she refuses even to leave her Southern town. Won't speak to, much less go down on, either of the two gays.

He races back and forth between an image of her bound and on her knees, to two black men and a white woman becoming acquainted outside a bar.

This does not help.

Besides, she is involved in the activity inside herself and holding him—nostalgically.

He feels himself sliding down the wall that is her body, and expelled from inside her.

ADVANCING
LUNA—
AND
IDA B. WELLS

I met Luna the summer of 1965 in Atlanta where we both attended a political conference and rally. It was designed to give us the courage, as temporary civil rights workers, to penetrate the small hamlets farther south. I had taken a bus from Sarah Lawrence in New York and gone back to Georgia, my home state, to try my hand at registering voters. It had become obvious from the high spirits and sense of almost divine purpose exhibited by black people that a revolution was going on, and I did not intend to miss it. Especially not this summery, student-studded version of it. And I thought it would be fun to spend some time on my own in the South.

Luna was sitting on the back of a pickup truck, waiting for someone to take her from Faith Baptist, where the rally was held, to whatever gracious black Negro home awaited her. I remember because someone who assumed

I would also be traveling by pickup introduced us. I remember her face when I said, "No, no more back of pickup trucks for me. I know Atlanta well enough, I'll walk." She assumed of course (I guess) that I did not wish to ride beside her because she was white, and I was not curious enough about what she might have thought to explain it to her. And yet I was struck by her passivity, her *patience* as she sat on the truck alone and ignored, because someone had told her to wait there quietly until it was time to go.

This look of passively waiting for something changed very little over the years I knew her. It was only four or five years in all that I did. It seems longer, perhaps because we met at such an optimistic time in our lives. John Kennedy and Malcolm X had already been assassinated, but King had not been and Bobby Kennedy had not been. Then too, the lethal, bizarre elimination by death of this militant or that, exiles, flights to Cuba, shoot-outs between former Movement friends sundered forever by lies planted by the FBI, the gunning down of Mrs. Martin Luther King, Sr., as she played the Lord's Prayer on the piano in her church (was her name Alberta?), were still in the happily unfathomable future.

We believed we could change America because we were young and bright and held ourselves *responsible* for changing it. We did not believe we would fail. That is what lent fervor (revivalist fervor, in fact; we would *revive* America!) to our songs, and lent sweetness to our friendships (in the beginning almost all interracial), and gave a wonderful fillip to our sex (which, too, in the beginning, was almost always interracial).

What first struck me about Luna when we later lived together was that she did not own a bra. This was curious to me, I suppose, because she also did not need one. Her chest was practically flat, her breasts like those of a child. Her face was round, and she suffered from acne. She carried with her always a tube of that "skin-colored" (if one's skin is pink or eggshell) medication designed to dry up pimples. At the oddest times—waiting for a light to change, listening to voter registration instructions, talking about her father's new girlfriend, she would apply the stuff, holding in her other hand a small brass mirror the size of her thumb, which she also carried for just this purpose.

We were assigned to work together in a small, rigidly segregated South Georgia town that the city fathers, incongruously and years ago, had named Freehold. Luna was slightly asthmatic and when overheated or nervous she breathed through her mouth. She wore her shoulder-length black hair with bangs to her eyebrows and the rest brushed behind her ears. Her eyes were brown and rather small. She was attractive, but just barely and with effort. Had she been the slightest bit overweight, for instance, she would have gone completely unnoticed, and would have faded into the background where, even in a revolution, fat people seem destined to go. I have a photograph of her sitting on the steps of a house in South Georgia. She is wearing tiny pearl earrings, a dark sleeveless shirt with Peter Pan collar, Bermuda shorts, and a pair of those East Indian sandals that seem to adhere to nothing but a big toe.

The summer of '65 was as hot as any other in that part of the South. There was an abundance of flies and mosquitoes. Everyone complained about the heat and the flies and the hard work, but Luna complained less than the rest of us. She walked ten miles a day with me up and down those straight Georgia highways, stopping at every house that looked black (one could always tell in 1965) and asking whether anyone needed help with learning how to vote. The simple mechanics: writing one's name, or making one's "X" in the proper column. And then, though we were required to walk, everywhere, we were empowered to offer prospective registrants a car in which they might safely ride down to the county courthouse. And later to the polling places. Luna, almost overcome by the heat, breathing through her mouth like a dog, her hair plastered with sweat to her head, kept looking straight ahead, and walking as if the walking itself was her reward.

I don't know if we accomplished much that summer. In retrospect, it seems not only minor, but irrelevant. A bunch of us, black and white, lived together. The black people who took us in were unfailingly hospitable and kind. I took them for granted in a way that now amazes me. I realize that at each and every house we visited I *assumed* hospitality, I *assumed* kindness. Luna was often startled by my "boldness." If we walked up to a secluded farmhouse and half a dozen dogs ran up barking around our heels and a large black man with a shotgun could be seen whistling to himself under a tree, she would become nervous. I, on the other hand, felt free to yell at this stranger's dogs, slap a couple of them on the nose, and call over to him about his hunting.

That month with Luna of approaching new black people every day taught me something about myself I had always suspected: I thought black people superior people. Not simply superior to white people, because even without thinking about it much, I assumed almost everyone was superior to them; but to everyone. Only white people, after all, would blow up a Sunday-school class and grin for television over their "victory," *i.e.*, the death of four small black girls. Any atrocity, at any time, was expected from them. On the other hand, it never occurred to me that black people *could* treat Luna and me with anything but warmth and concern. Even their curiosity about the sudden influx into their midst of rather ignorant white and black Northerners was restrained and courteous. I was treated as a relative, Luna as a much welcomed guest.

Luna and I were taken in by a middle-aged couple and

their young school-age daughter. The mother worked outside the house in a local canning factory, the father worked
in the paper plant in nearby Augusta. Never did they
speak of the danger they were in of losing their jobs over
keeping us, and never did their small daughter show any
fear that her house might be attacked by racists because
we were there. Again, I did not expect this family to complain, no matter what happened to them because of us.
Having understood the danger, they had assumed the risk.
I did not think them particularly brave, merely typical.

I think Luna liked the smallness—only four rooms—of
the house. It was in this house that she ridiculed her
mother's lack of taste. Her yellow-and-mauve house in
Cleveland, the eleven rooms, the heated garage, the new
car every year, her father's inability to remain faithful to
her mother, their divorce, the fight over the property, even
more bitter than over the children. Her mother kept the
house and the children. Her father kept the car and his
new girlfriend, whom he wanted Luna to meet and "ap-
prove." I could hardly imagine anyone disliking her
mother so much. Everything Luna hated in her she
summed up in three words: *"yellow and mauve."*

I have a second photograph of Luna and a group of us
being bullied by a Georgia state trooper. This member of
Georgia's finest had followed us out into the deserted
countryside to lecture us on how misplaced—in the South
—was our energy, when "the Lord knew" the North
(where he thought all of us lived, expressing disbelief that
most of us were Georgians) was just as bad. (He had a
point that I recognized even then, but it did not seem the
point where we were.) Luna is looking up at him, her
mouth slightly open as always, a somewhat dazed look on
her face. I cannot detect fear on any of our faces, though
we were all afraid. After all, 1965 was only a year after
1964 when three civil rights workers had been taken deep
into a Mississippi forest by local officials and sadistically

tortured and murdered. Luna almost always carried a flat black shoulder bag. She is standing with it against her side, her thumb in the strap.

At night we slept in the same bed. We talked about our schools, lovers, girlfriends we didn't understand or missed. She dreamed, she said, of going to Goa. I dreamed of going to Africa. My dream came true earlier than hers: an offer of a grant from an unsuspected source reached me one day as I was writing poems under a tree. I left Freehold, Georgia, in the middle of summer, without regrets, and flew from New York to London, to Cairo, to Kenya, and, finally, to Uganda, where I settled among black people with the same assumptions of welcome and kindness I had taken for granted in Georgia. I was taken on rides down the Nile as a matter of course, and accepted all invitations to dinner, where the best local dishes were superbly prepared in my honor. I became, in fact, a lost relative of the people, whose ancestors had foolishly strayed, long ago, to America.

I wrote to Luna at once.

But I did not see her again for almost a year. I had graduated from college, moved into a borrowed apartment in Brooklyn Heights, and was being evicted after a month. Luna, living then in a tenement on East 9th Street, invited me to share her two-bedroom apartment. If I had seen the apartment before the day I moved in I might never have agreed to do so. Her building was between Avenues B and C and did not have a front door. Junkies, winos, and others often wandered in during the night (and occasionally during the day) to sleep underneath the stairs or to relieve themselves at the back of the first-floor hall.

Luna's apartment was on the third floor. Everything in it was painted white. The contrast between her three rooms and kitchen (with its red bathtub) and the grungy stairway was stunning. Her furniture consisted of two large brass beds inherited from a previous tenant and stripped of paint by Luna, and a long, high-backed church pew which she had managed somehow to bring up from the South. There was a simplicity about the small apartment that I liked. I also liked the notion of extreme contrast, and I do to this day. Outside our front window was the decaying neighborhood, as ugly and ill-lit as a battleground. (And allegedly as hostile, though somehow we were never threatened with bodily harm by the Hispanics who were our neighbors, and who seemed, more than anything, *bewildered* by the darkness and filth of their surroundings.) Inside was the church pew, as straight and spare as Abe Lincoln lying down, the white walls as spotless as a monastery's, and a small, unutterably pure patch of blue sky through the window of the back bedroom. (Luna did not believe in curtains, or couldn't afford them, and so we always undressed and bathed with the lights off and the rooms lit with candles, causing rather nun-shaped shadows to be cast on the walls by the long-sleeved high-necked nightgowns we both wore to bed.)

Over a period of weeks, our relationship, always marked by mutual respect, evolved into a warm and comfortable friendship which provided a stability and comfort we both needed at that time. I had taken a job at the Welfare Department during the day, and set up my typewriter permanently in the tiny living room for work after I got home. Luna worked in a kindergarten, and in the evenings taught herself Portuguese.

It was while we lived on East 9th Street that she told me she had been raped during her summer in the South. It is hard for me, even now, to relate my feeling of horror and incredulity. This was some time before Eldridge Cleaver wrote of being a rapist / revolutionary; of "practicing" on black women before moving on to white. It was also, unless I'm mistaken, before LeRoi Jones (as he was then known; now of course Imamu Baraka, which has an even more presumptuous meaning than "the King") wrote his advice to young black male insurrectionaries (women were not told what to do with *their* rebelliousness): "Rape the white girls. Rape their fathers." It was clear that he meant this literally and also as: to rape a white girl *is* to rape her father. It was the misogynous cruelty of this latter meaning that was habitually lost on black men (on men in general, actually), but nearly always perceived and rejected by women of whatever color.

"Details?" I asked.

She shrugged. Gave his name. A name recently in the news, though in very small print.

He was not a Movement star or anyone you would know. We had met once, briefly. I had not liked him because he was coarse and spoke of black women as "our" women. (In the early Movement, it was pleasant to think of black men wanting to own us as a group; later it became clear that owning us meant exactly *that* to them.) He was physically unattractive, I had thought, with something of the hoodlum about him: a swaggering, unnecessarily mobile walk, small eyes, rough skin, a mouthful of wandering or absent teeth. He was, ironically, among the first persons to shout the slogan everyone later attributed solely to Stokeley Carmichael—Black Power! Stokeley was chosen as the originator of this idea by the media, because he was physically beautiful and photogenic and articulate. Even the name—Freddie Pye—was diminutive, I thought, in an age of giants.

"What did you do?"

"Nothing that required making a noise."

"Why didn't you scream?" I felt I would have screamed my head off.

"You know why."

I did. I had seen a photograph of Emmett Till's body just after it was pulled from the river. I had seen photographs of white folks standing in a circle roasting something that had talked to them in their own language before they tore out its tongue. I knew why, all right.

"What was he trying to prove?"

"I don't know. Do you?"

"Maybe you filled him with unendurable lust," I said.

"I don't think so," she said.

Suddenly I was embarrassed. Then angry. Very, very angry. *How dare she tell me this!* I thought.

Who knows what the black woman thinks of rape? Who has asked her? Who *cares*? Who has even properly acknowledged that *she* and not the white woman in this story is the most likely victim of rape? Whenever interracial rape is mentioned, a black woman's first thought is to protect the lives of her brothers, her father, her sons, her lover. A history of lynching has bred this reflex in her. I feel it as strongly as anyone. While writing a fictional account of such a rape in a novel, I read Ida B. Wells's autobiography three times, as a means of praying to her spirit to forgive me.

My prayer, as I turned the pages, went like this: *"Please forgive me. I am a writer."* (This self-revealing statement alone often seems to me sufficient reason to require perpetual forgiveness; since the writer is guilty not only of always wanting to know—like Eve—but also of trying—again like Eve—to find out.) *"I cannot write contrary to what life reveals to me. I wish to malign no one. But I must struggle to understand at least my own tangled emotions about interracial rape. I know, Ida B. Wells, you spent your whole life protecting, and trying to protect, black men accused of raping white women, who were lynched by white mobs, or threatened with it. You know, better than I ever will, what it means for a whole people to live under the terror of lynching. Under the slander that their men, where white women are concerned, are crea-*

*tures of uncontrollable sexual lust. You made it so clear
that the black men accused of rape in the past were innocent victims of white criminals that I grew up believing
black men literally did not rape white women. At all. Ever.
Now it would appear that some of them, the very twisted,
the terribly ill, do. What would you have me write about
them?"*

Her answer was: *"Write nothing. Nothing at all. It will
be used against black men and therefore against all of us.
Eldridge Cleaver and LeRoi Jones don't know who they're
dealing with. But you remember. You are dealing with
people who brought their children to witness the murder
of black human beings, falsely accused of rape. People who
handed out, as trophies, black fingers and toes. Deny! Deny!
Deny!"*

And yet, I have pursued it: *"Some black men themselves
do not seem to know what the meaning of raping someone
is. Some have admitted rape in order to denounce it, but
others have accepted rape as a part of rebellion, of 'paying
whitey back.' They have gloried in it."*

"They know nothing of America," she says. *"And neither, apparently, do you. No matter what you think you
know, no matter what you feel about it, say nothing. And
to your dying breath!"*

Which, to my mind, is virtually useless advice to give to
a writer.

Freddie Pye was the kind of man I would not have looked
at then, not even once. (Throughout that year I was more
or less into exotica: white ethnics who knew languages
were a peculiar weakness; a half-white hippie singer; also
a large Chinese mathematician who was a marvelous dancer
and who taught me to waltz.) There was no question of
belief.

But, in retrospect, there was a momentary *suspension* of
belief, a kind of *hope* that perhaps it had not really hap-

pened; that Luna had made up the rape, "as white women have been wont to do." I soon realized this was unlikely. I was the only person she had told.

She looked at me as if to say: "I'm glad *that* part of my life is over." We continued our usual routine. We saw every interminable, foreign, depressing, and poorly illuminated film ever made. We learned to eat brown rice and yogurt and to tolerate kasha and odd-tasting teas. My half-black hippie singer friend (now a well-known reggae singer who says he is from "de I-lands" and not Sheepshead Bay) was "into" tea and kasha and Chinese vegetables.

And yet the rape, the knowledge of the rape, out in the open, admitted, pondered over, was now between us. (And I began to think that perhaps—whether Luna had been raped or not—it had always been so; that her power over my life was exactly the power *her word on rape* had over the lives of black men, over *all* black men, whether they were guilty or not, and therefore over my whole people.)

Before she told me about the rape, I think we had assumed a lifelong friendship. The kind of friendship one dreams of having with a person one has known in adversity; under heat and mosquitoes and immaturity and the threat of death. We would each travel, we would write to each other from the three edges of the world.

We would continue to have an "international list" of lovers whose amorous talents or lack of talents we would continue (giggling into our dotage) to compare. Our friendship would survive everything, be truer than everything, endure even our respective marriages, children, husbands—assuming we *did*, out of desperation and boredom someday, marry, which did not seem a probability, exactly, but more in the area of an amusing idea.

But now there was a cooling off of our affection for each other. Luna was becoming mildly interested in drugs, because everyone we knew was. I was envious of the open-endedness of her life. The financial backing to it. When

she left her job at the kindergarten because she was tired
of working, her errant father immediately materialized.
He took her to dine on scampi at an expensive restaurant,
scolded her for living on East 9th Street, and looked at me
as if to say: "Living in a slum of this magnitude must
surely have been your idea." As a cullud, of course.

For me there was the welfare department every day,
attempting to get the necessary food and shelter to people
who would always live amid the dirty streets I knew I
must soon leave. I was, after all, a Sarah Lawrence girl
"with talent." It would be absurd to rot away in a building that had no front door.

I slept late one Sunday morning with a painter I had met
at the Welfare Department. A man who looked for all the
world like Gene Autry, the singing cowboy, but who
painted wonderful surrealist pictures of birds and ghouls
and fruit with *teeth*. The night before, three of us—me,
the painter, and "an old Navy buddy" who looked like his
twin and who had just arrived in town—had got high on
wine and grass.

That morning the Navy buddy snored outside the bed-
rooms like a puppy waiting for its master. Luna got up
early, made an immense racket getting breakfast, scowled
at me as I emerged from my room, and left the apartment,
slamming the door so hard she damaged the lock. (Luna
had made it a rule to date black men almost exclusively.
My insistence on dating, as she termed it, "anyone" was
incomprehensible to her, since in a politically diseased
society to "sleep with the enemy" was to become "infected"
with the enemy's "political germs." There is more than a
grain of truth in this, of course, but I was having too much
fun to stare at it for long. Still, coming from Luna it was
amusing, since she never took into account the risk her
own black lovers ran by sleeping with "the white woman,"
and she had apparently been convinced that a summer of

relatively innocuous political work in the South had cured her of any racial, economic, or sexual political disease.)

Luna never told me what irked her so that Sunday morning, yet I remember it as the end of our relationship. It was not, as I at first feared, that she thought my bringing the two men to the apartment was inconsiderate. The way we lived allowed us to *be* inconsiderate from time to time. Our friends were varied, vital, and often strange. Her friends especially were deeper than they should have been into drugs.

The distance between us continued to grow. She talked more of going to Goa. My guilt over my dissolute if pleasurable existence coupled with my mounting hatred of welfare work, propelled me in two directions: south and to West Africa. When the time came to choose, I discovered that *my* summer in the South had infected me with the need to return, to try to understand, and write about, the people I'd merely lived with before.

We never discussed the rape again. We never discussed, really, Freddie Pye or Luna's remaining feelings about what had happened. One night, the last month we lived together, I noticed a man's blue denim jacket thrown across the church pew. The next morning, out of Luna's bedroom walked Freddie Pye. He barely spoke to me— possibly because as a black woman I was expected to be hostile toward his presence in a white woman's bedroom. I was too surprised to exhibit hostility, however, which was only a part of what I felt, after all. He left.

Luna and I did not discuss this. It is odd, I think now, that we didn't. It was as if he was never there, as if he and Luna had not shared the bedroom that night. A month later, Luna went alone to Goa, in her solitary way. She lived on an island and slept, she wrote, on the beach. She mentioned she'd found a lover there who protected her from the local beachcombers and pests.

Several years later, she came to visit me in the South

and brought a lovely piece of pottery which my daughter much later dropped and broke, but which I glued back together in such a way that the flaw improves the beauty and fragility of the design.

Afterwords, Afterwards
Second Thoughts

That is the "story." It has an "unresolved" ending. That is because Freddie Pye and Luna are still alive, as am I. However, one evening while talking to a friend, I heard myself say that I had, in fact, written *two* endings. One, which follows, I considered appropriate for such a story published in a country truly committed to justice, and the one above, which is the best I can afford to offer a society in which lynching is still reserved, at least subconsciously, as a means of racial control.

I said that if we in fact lived in a society committed to the establishment of justice for everyone ("justice" in this case encompassing equal housing, education, access to work, adequate dental care, et cetera), thereby placing Luna and Freddie Pye in their correct relationship to each other, *i.e.*, that of brother and sister, *compañeros*, then the two of them would be required to struggle together over what his rape of her had meant.

Since my friend is a black man whom I love and who loves me, we spent a considerable amount of time discussing what this particular rape meant to us. Morally wrong, we said, and not to be excused. Shameful; politically corrupt. Yet, as we thought of what might have happened to an indiscriminate number of innocent young black men in Freehold, Georgia, had Luna screamed, it became clear that more than a little of Ida B. Wells's fear of probing the rape issue was running through us, too. The implications of this fear would not let me rest, so that months and years went by with most of the story written but with me incapable, or at least unwilling, to finish or to publish it.

In thinking about it over a period of years, there occurred a number of small changes, refinements, puzzles, in angle. Would these shed a wider light on the continuing subject? I do not know. In any case, I returned to my notes, hereto appended for the use of the reader.

Luna: Ida B. Wells—Discarded Notes

Additional characteristics of Luna: At a time when many in and out of the Movement considered "nigger" and "black" synonymous, and indulged in a sincere attempt to fake Southern "hip" speech, Luna resisted. She was the kind of WASP who could not easily imitate another's ethnic style, nor could she even exaggerate her own. She was what she was. A very straight, clear-eyed, coolly observant young woman with no talent for existing outside her own skin.

Imaginary Knowledge

Luna explained the visit from Freddie Pye in this way:
"He called that evening, said he was in town, and did I know the Movement was coming north? I replied that I did know that."
When could he see her? he wanted to know.
"Never," she replied.
He had burst into tears, or something that sounded like tears, over the phone. He was stranded at wherever the evening's fund-raising event had been held. Not in the place itself, but outside, in the street. The "stars" had left, everyone had left. He was alone. He knew no one else in the city. Had found her number in the phone book. And had no money, no place to stay.
Could he, he asked, crash? He was tired, hungry, broke

—and even in the South had had no job, other than the Movement, for months. Et cetera.

When he arrived, she had placed our only steak knife in the waistband of her jeans.

He had asked for a drink of water. She gave him orange juice, some cheese, and a couple of slices of bread. She had told him he might sleep on the church pew and he had lain down with his head on his rolled-up denim jacket. She had retired to her room, locked the door, and tried to sleep. She was amazed to discover herself worrying that the church pew was both too narrow and too hard.

At first he muttered, groaned, and cursed in his sleep. Then he fell off the narrow church pew. He kept rolling off. At two in the morning she unlocked her door, showed him her knife, and invited him to share her bed.

Nothing whatever happened except they talked. At first, only he talked. Not about the rape, but about his life.

"He was a small person physically, remember?" Luna asked me. (She was right. Over the years he had grown big and, yes, burly, in my imagination, and I'm sure in hers.) "That night he seemed tiny. A child. He was still fully dressed, except for the jacket and he, literally, hugged his side of the bed. I hugged mine. The whole bed, in fact, was between us. We were merely hanging to its edges."

At the fund-raiser—on Fifth Avenue and 71st Street, as it turned out—his leaders had introduced him as the un-skilled, barely literate, former Southern fieldworker that he was. They had pushed him at the rich people gathered there as an example of what "the system" did to "the little people" in the South. They asked him to tell about the thirty-seven times he had been jailed. The thirty-five times he had been beaten. The one time he had lost conscious-ness in the "hot" box. They told him not to worry about his grammar. "Which, as you may recall," said Luna, "was horrible." Even so, he had tried to censor his "ain'ts" and his "us'es." He had been painfully aware that he was on

*exhibit, like Frederick Douglass had been for the Aboli-
tionists. But unlike Douglass he had no oratorical gift, no
passionate language, no silver tongue. He knew the rich
people and his own leaders perceived he was nothing: a
broken man, unschooled, unskilled at anything. . . .*

*Yet he had spoken, trembling before so large a crowd of
rich, white Northerners—who clearly thought their section of the country would never have the South's racial
problems—begging, with the painful stories of his wretched
life, for their money.*

*At the end, all of them—the black leaders, too—had
gone. They left him watching the taillights of their cars,
recalling the faces of the friends come to pick them up:
the women dressed in African print that shone, with elab-
orately arranged hair, their jewelry sparkling, their perfume exotic. They were so beautiful, yet so strange. He
could not imagine that one of them could comprehend
his life. He did not ask for a ride, because of that, but also
because he had no place to go. Then he had remembered
Luna.*

*Soon Luna would be required to talk. She would men-
tion her confusion over whether, in a black community
surrounded by whites with a history of lynching blacks,
she had a right to scream as Freddie Pye was raping her.
For her, this was the crux of the matter.*

And so they would continue talking through the night.

This is another ending, created from whole cloth. If I
believed Luna's story about the rape, and I did (had she
told anyone else I might have dismissed it), then this
reconstruction of what might have happened is as prob-
able an accounting as any is liable to be. Two people have
now become "characters."

I have forced them to talk until they reached the stum-
bling block of the rape, *which they must remove themselves*, before proceeding to a place from which it will be

possible to insist on a society in which Luna's word alone on rape can never be used to intimidate an entire people, and in which an innocent black man's protestation of innocence of rape is unprejudicially heard. Until such a society is created, relationships of affection between black men and white women will always be poisoned—from within as from without—by historical fear and the threat of violence, and solidarity among black and white women is only rarely likely to exist.

Postscript: Havana, Cuba, November 1976

I am in Havana with a group of other black American artists. We have spent the morning apart from our Cuban hosts bringing each other up to date on the kind of work (there are no apolitical artists among us) we are doing in the United States. I have read "Luna."

High above the beautiful city of Havana I sit in the Havana Libre pavilion with the muralist / photographer in our group. He is in his mid-thirties, a handsome, brown, erect individual whom I have known casually for a number of years. During the sixties he designed and painted street murals for both SNCC and the Black Panthers, and in an earlier discussion with Cuban artists he showed impatience with their explanation of why we had seen no murals covering some of the city's rather dingy walls: Cuba, they had said, unlike Mexico, has no mural tradition. "But the point of a revolution," insisted Our Muralist, "is to make new traditions!" And he had pressed his argument with such passion for the *usefulness*, for revolutionary communication, of his craft, that the Cubans were both exasperated and impressed. They drove us around the city for a tour of their huge billboards, all advancing socialist thought and the heroism of men like Lenin, Camilo, and Che Guevara, and said, "These, *these* are our 'murals'!"

While we ate lunch, I asked Our Muralist what he'd thought of "Luna." Especially the appended section.

"Not much," was his reply. "Your view of human weakness is too biblical," he said. "You are unable to conceive of the man without conscience. The man who cares nothing about the state of his soul because he's long since sold it. In short," he said, "you do not understand that some people are simply evil, a disease on the lives of other people, and that to remove the disease altogether is preferable to trying to interpret, contain, or forgive it. Your 'Freddie Pye,' " and he laughed, "was probably raping white women on the instructions of his government."

Oh ho, I thought. Because, of course, for a second, during which I stalled my verbal reply, this comment made both very little and very much sense.

"I *am* sometimes naive and sentimental," I offered. I am sometimes both, though frequently by design. Admission in this way is tactical, a stimulant to conversation.

"And shocked at what I've said," he said, and laughed again. "Even though," he continued, "you know by now that blacks could be hired to blow up other blacks, and could be hired *by someone* to shoot down Brother Malcolm, and hired *by someone* to provide a diagram of Fred Hampton's bedroom so the pigs could shoot him easily while he slept, you find it hard to believe a black man could be hired *by someone* to rape white women. But think a minute, and you will see why it is the perfect disruptive act. Enough blacks raping or accused of raping enough white women and any political movement that cuts across racial lines is doomed.

"Larger forces are at work than your story would indicate," he continued. "You're still thinking of lust and rage, moving slowly into aggression and purely racial hatred. But you should be considering money—which the rapist would get, probably from your very own tax dollars, in fact—and a maintaining of the status quo; which those

---

103

hiring the rapist would achieve. I know all this," he said, "because when I was broke and hungry and selling my blood to buy the food and the paint that allowed me to work, I was offered such 'other work.' "

"But you did not take it."

He frowned. "There you go again. How do you know I didn't take it? It paid, and I was starving."

"You didn't take it," I repeated.

"No," he said. "A black and white 'team' made the offer. I had enough energy left to threaten to throw them out of the room."

"But even if Freddie Pye *had been* hired *by someone* to rape Luna, that still would not explain his second visit."

"Probably nothing will explain that," said Our Muralist. "But assuming Freddie Pye *was* paid to disrupt—by raping a white woman—the black struggle in the South, he may have wised up enough later to comprehend the significance of Luna's decision not to scream."

"So you are saying he *did have* a conscience?" I asked.

"Maybe," he said, but his look clearly implied I would never understand anything about evil, power, or corrupted human beings in the modern world.

But of course he is wrong.

LAUREL

It was during that summer in the mid-sixties that I met Laurel.

There was a new radical Southern newspaper starting up . . . it was only six months old at the time, and was called *First Rebel.* The title referred, of course, to the black slave who was rebelling all over the South long before the white rebels fought the Civil War. Laurel was in Atlanta to confer with the young people on its staff, and, since he wished to work on a radical, racially mixed newspaper himself, to see if perhaps *First Rebel* might be it.

I was never interested in working on a newspaper, however radical. I agree with Leonard Woolf that to write against a weekly deadline deforms the brain. Still, I attended several of the editorial meetings of *First Rebel* because while wandering out of the first one, fleeing it, in fact, I'd bumped into Laurel, who, squinting at me through cheap, fingerprint-smudged blue-and-gray-framed bifocals, asked if I knew where the meeting was.

He seemed a parody of the country hick; he was tall, slightly stooped, with blackish hair cut exactly as if someone had put a bowl over his head. Even his ears stuck out, and were large and pink.

Really, I thought.

Though he was no more than twenty-two, two years older than me, he seemed older. No doubt his bifocals added to this impression, as did his nonchalant gait and slouchy posture. His eyes were clear and brown and filled with an appropriate country slyness. It was his voice that held me. It had a charming lilt to it.

"Would you say that again?" I asked.

"Sure," he said, making it two syllables, the last syllable a higher pitch than the first. "I'm looking for where *First Rebel*, the newspaper, is meeting. What are *you* doing?"

The country slyness was clumsily replaced by a look of country seduction.

Have mercy! I thought. And burst into laughter.

Laurel grinned, his ears reddening.

And so we became involved in planning a newspaper that was committed to combating racism and other violence in the South . . . (until it ran out of funds and folded three years and many pieces of invaluable investigative journalism later).

Laurel's was not a variation of a Southern accent, as I'd at first thought. His ancestors had immigrated to the United States in the early 1800s. They had settled in California because there they found the two things they liked best: wine grapes and apples.

I'd never heard anything like Laurel's speech. He could ask a question like "How d'you happen t' be here?" and it sounded as if two happy but languid children were slowly jumping rope under apple trees in the sun. And on

Laurel himself, while he spoke, I seemed to smell apples and the faint woodruffy bouquet of May wine.

He was also effortlessly complimentary. He would say, as we went through the cafeteria line, "You're beaut-ti-ful, reel-i," and it was like hearing it and caring about hearing it for the first time. Laurel, who loved working among the grapes, and had done so up to the moment of leaving the orchards for Atlanta, had dirt, lots of it, under his nails.

That's it, I thought. I can safely play here. No one brings such dirty nails home to dinner. That was Monday. By Tuesday I thought that dirty nails were just the right nonbourgeois attribute and indicated a lack of personal concern for appearances that included the smudged bifocals and the frazzled but beautifully fitting jeans; in a back pocket of which was invariably a half-rolled, impressively battered paperback book. It occurred to me that I could not look at Laurel without wanting to make love with him.

He was the same.

For a while, I blamed it on Atlanta in the spring . . . the cherry trees that blossomed around the campus buildings, the wonderful honeysuckle smells of our South, the excitement of being far away from New York City and its never-to-be-gotten-used-to dirt. But it was more: if we both walked into a room from separate doors, even if we didn't see each other, a current dragged us together. At breakfast neither of us could eat, except chokingly, so intense was our longing to be together. Minus people, table, food.

A veritable movie.

Throughout the rest of the week we racked our brains trying to think of a place to make love. But the hotels were still segregated, and once, after a Movement party at somebody's house, we were severely reprimanded for walking out into the Southern night, blissfully hand in hand.

"Don't you know this is outrageous?" a young black man asked us, pulling us into his car, where I sat on

Laurel's lap in a kind of sensual stupor—hearing his words, agreeing with them, knowing the bloody History behind them . . . but not caring in the least.

In short, there was no place for us to make love, as that term is popularly understood. We were housed in dormitories. Men in one. Women in another. Interracial couples were under surveillance wherever the poor things raised their heads anywhere in the city. We were reduced to a kind of sexual acrobatics on a bench close beside one of the dormitories. And, as lovers know, acrobatics of a sexual sort puts a strain on one's powers of physical ingenuity while making one's lust all the more a resident of the brain, where it quickly becomes all-pervading, insatiable, and profound.

The state of lust itself is not a happy one if there is no relief in sight. Though I am happy enough to enter that state whenever it occurs, I have learned to acknowledge its many and often devastating limitations. For example, the most monumental issues fade from one's consciousness as if erased by a swift wind. Movements of great social and political significance seem but backdrops to one's daily exchanges—be they ever so muted and circumscribed— with the Object of One's Desire. (I at least was not yet able to articulate how the personal is the political, as was certainly true in Laurel's and my case. Viz., nobody wanted us to go to bed with each other, except us, and they had made laws to that effect. And of course whether we slept together or not was nobody's business, except ours.)

The more it became impossible to be with Laurel, to make love fully and naturally, the more I wanted nothing but that. If the South had risen again during one of our stolen kisses—his hands on my breasts, my hands on his (his breasts were sensitive, we discovered quite by acrobatic invention and accident)—we would have been hard pressed to notice. This is "criminal" to write, of course, given the myths that supposedly make multiracial living so much easier to bear, but it is quite true. And yet, after our week together—passionate, beautiful, haunting, and never, never to be approximated between us again, our desire to make love never to be fulfilled (though we did not know this then), we went our separate ways. Because in fact, while we kissed and said Everything Else Be Damned! the South *was* rising again. *Was* murdering people. Was imprisoning our colleagues and friends. Was keeping us from strolling off to a clean, cheap hotel.

It was during our last night together that he told me about his wife. We were dancing in a local Movement-oriented nightclub. What would today be called a disco. He had an endearing way of dancing, even to slow tunes (during which we clung together shamelessly); he did a sort of hop, fast or slow depending on the music, from one foot to the other, almost in time with the music—and that was dance to him. It didn't bother me at all. Our bodies easily found their own rhythms anyway, and touching alone was our reason for being on the floor. *There* we could make a sort of love, in a dark enough corner, that was not exactly grace but was not, was definitely not, acrobatics.

He peered at me through the gray-and-blue-framed glasses.

"I've got a wife back home."

What I've most resented as "the other woman" is being made responsible for the continued contentment and happiness of the wife. On our last night together, our lust undiminished and apparently not to be extinguished, given our surroundings, what was I supposed to do with this information?

All I could think was: She's not *my* wife.

She was, from what little he said, someone admirable. She was away from home for the summer, studying for an advanced degree. He seemed perplexed by this need of hers to continue her education instead of settling down to have his children, but lonely rather than bitter.

So it was *just sex* between us, after all, I thought.

(To be fair, I was engaged to a young man in the Peace Corps. I didn't mind if it *was* just sex, since by that time our mutual lust had reached a state, almost, of mysticism.)

Laurel, however, was tormented.

(I never told him about my engagement. As far as I was concerned, it remained to be seen whether my engagement was relevant to my relationships with others. I thought not, but realized I was still quite young.)

That night, Laurel wrung his hands, pulled his strangely cut hair and cried, as we brazenly walked out along Atlanta's dangerous, cracker-infested streets.

I cried because he did, and because in some odd way it relieved my lust. Besides, I enjoyed watching myself pretend to suffer. . . . Such moments of emotional dishonesty are always paid for, however, and that I did not know this at the time attests to my willingness to believe our relationship would not live past the moment itself.

And yet.

There was one letter from him to me after I'd settled in a small Georgia town (a) to picket the jailhouse where a local schoolteacher was under arrest for picketing the jailhouse where a local parent was under arrest for picketing the jailhouse where a local child was under arrest for picketing . . . and (b) to register voters.

He wrote that he missed me.

I missed him. He was the principal other actor in all my fantasies. I wrote him that I was off to Africa, but would continue to write. I gave him the address of my school, to which he could send letters.

Once in Africa, my fiancé (who was conveniently in the next country from mine and free to visit) and I completed a breakup that had been coming for our entire two-year period of engagement. He told me, among other things, that it was not uncommon for Peace Corps men to sleep with ten-year-old African girls. *At that age, you see, they were still attractive.* I wrote about that aspect of the Peace Corps' activities to Laurel, as if I'd heard about it from a stranger.

Laurel, I felt, would never take advantage of a ten-year-old child. And I loved him for it.

Loving him, I was not prepared for the absence of letters from him, back at my school. Three months after my return I still had heard nothing. Out of depression over this and the distraction schoolwork provided, I was a practicing celibate. Only rarely did I feel lustful, and then of course I always thought of Laurel, as of a great opportunity, much missed. I thought of his musical speech and his scent of apples and May wine with varying degrees of regret and tenderness. However, our week of passion—magical, memorable, but far too brief—gradually assumed a less than central place even in my most sanguine recollections.

In late November, six months after Laurel and I met, I received a letter from his wife.

My first thought, when I saw the envelope, was: She has the same last name as his. It was the first time their marriage was real for me. I was also frightened that she wrote to accuse me of disturbing her peace. Why else would a wife write?

She wrote that on July fourth of the previous summer (six weeks after Laurel and I met) Laurel had had an automobile accident. He was driving his van, delivering copies of *First Rebel*. He had either fallen asleep at the wheel or been run off the road by local rebels of the other kind. He had sustained a broken leg, a fractured back, and a severely damaged brain. He had been in a coma for the past four months. Nothing could rouse him. She had found my letter in his pocket. Perhaps I would come see him?

(I was never to meet Laurel's wife, but I admired this gesture then, and I admire it now.)

It was a small Catholic hospital in Laurel's hometown. In the entryway a bloody, gruesome, ugly Christ the color of a rutabaga, stood larger than life. Nuns dressed in black and white habits reminded one of giant flies. Floating moonlike above their "wings," their pink, cherubic faces were kind and comical.

Laurel's father looked very much like Laurel. The same bifocals, the same plain clothing, the same open-seeming face—but on closer look, wide rather than open. The same lilt to his voice. Laurel's sister was also there. She, unaccountably, embraced me.

"We're so glad you came," she said.

She was like Laurel too. Smaller, pretty, with short blond hair and apple cheeks.

She reached down and took Laurel's hand.

Laurel alone did not look like Laurel. He who had been healthy, firm-fleshed, virile, lay now on his hospital bed a skeleton with eyes. Tubes entered his body everywhere. His head was shaved, a bandage covering the hole that had been drilled in the top. His breathing was hardly a whistle through a hole punched in his throat.

I took the hands that had given such pleasure to my breasts, and they were bones, unmoving, cold, in mine. I touched the face I'd dreamed about for months as I would the face of someone already in a coffin.

His sister said, "Annie is here," her voice carrying the lilt.

Laurel's eyes were open, jerking, twitching, in his head. His mouth was open. But he was not there. Only his husk, his shell. His father looked at me—as he would look at any other treatment. Speculatively. Will it work? Will it revive my son?

I did not work. I did not revive his son. Laurel lay,

wheezing through the hole in his throat, helpless, insensate. I was eager to leave.

Two years later, the letters began to arrive. Exactly as if he thought I still waited for them at my school.

"My darling," he wrote, "I am loving you. Missing you and out of coma after a year and everybody given up on me. My brain damaged. Can you come to me? I am still bedridden."

But I was not in school. I was married, living in the South.

"Tell him you're married now," my husband advised. "He should know not to hurt himself with dreaming."

I wrote that I was not only married but "happily."

My marital status meant nothing to Laurel.

"Please come," he wrote. "There are few black people here. You would be lonesome but I will be here loving you."

I wrote again. This time I reported I was married, pregnant, and had a dog for protection.

"I dream of your body so luscious and fertile. I want so much to make love to you as we never could do. I hope you know how I lost part of my brain working for your people in the South. I miss you. Come soon."

I wrote: "Dear Laurel, I am so glad you are better. I'm sorry you were hurt. So sorry. I cannot come to you because I am married. I love my husband. I cannot bear to come. I am pregnant—nauseous all the time and anxious because of the life I/We lead." Etc., etc.

To which he replied: "You married a jew. [I had published a novel and apparently reviewers had focused on my marriage instead of my work as they often did.] There are no jews here either. I guess you have a taste for the exotic though I was not exotic. I am a cripple now with part of my brain in somebody's wastepaper basket. We

—

could have children if you will take the responsibility for
bringing them up. I cannot be counted on. Ha Ha."

I asked my husband to intercept the letters that came
to our house. I asked the president of my college to collect
and destroy those sent to me there. I dreaded seeing them.

"I dream of your body, so warm and brown, whereas
mine is white and cold to me now. I could take you as my
wife here the people are prejudiced against blacks they
were happy martin luther king was killed. I want you here.
We can be happy and black and beautiful and crippled
and missing part of my brain together. I want you but I
guess you are tied up with that jew husband of yours. I
mean no disrespect to him but we belong together you
know that."

"Dear Laurel, I am a mother. [I hoped this would save
me. It didn't.] I have a baby daughter. I hope you are well.
My husband sends his regards."

Most of Laurel's letters I was not shown. Assuming that
my husband confiscated his letters without my consent,
Laurel telegraphed: ANNIE, I AM COMING BY GREYHOUND
BUS DON'T LET YOUR DOG BITE ME, LAUREL.

My husband said: "Fine, let him come. Let him see
that you are not the woman he remembers. His memory
is frozen on your passion for each other. Let him see how
happy you and I are."

I waited, trembling.

It was a cold, clear evening. Laurel hobbled out of the
taxi on crutches, one leg shorter than the other. He had
regained his weight and, though pale, was almost handsome. He glanced at my completely handsome husband
once and dismissed him. He kept his eyes on me. He smiled
on me happily, pleased with me.

I knew only one dish then, chicken tarragon; I served it.

I was frightened. Not of Laurel, exactly, but of feeling
all the things I felt.

(My husband's conviction notwithstanding, I suspected

marriage could not keep me from being, in some ways, exactly the woman Laurel remembered.)

I woke up my infant daughter and held her, disgruntled, flushed and ludicrously alert, in front of me.

While we ate, Laurel urged me to recall our acrobatic nights on the dormitory bench, our intimate dancing. Before my courteous husband, my cheeks flamed. Those nights that seemed so far away to me seemed all he clearly remembered; he recalled less well how his accident occurred. Everything before and after that week had been swept away. The moment was real to him. I was real to him. Our week together long ago was very real to him. But that was all. His speech was as beautifully lilting as ever, with a zaniness that came from a lack of connective knowledge. But he was hard to listen to: he was both overconfident of his success with me—based on what he recalled of our mutual passion—and so intense that his gaze had me on the verge of tears.

Now that he was here and almost well, I must drop everything, including the baby on my lap—whom he barely seemed to see—and come away with him. Had I not flown off to Africa, though it meant leaving the very country in which he lived?

Finally, after the riddles within riddles that his words became (and not so much riddles as poems, and disturbing ones), my husband drove Laurel back to the bus station. He had come over a thousand miles for a two-hour visit.

My husband's face was drawn when he returned. He loved me, I was sure of that. He was glad to help me out. Still, he wondered.

"*It lasted a week!*" I said. "Long before I met you!"

"I know," he said. "Sha, sha, baby," he comforted me. I had crept into his arms, trembling from head to foot. "It's all right. We're safe."

But *were we?*

And Laurel? Zooming through the night back to his

home? The letters continued. Sometimes I asked to read one that came to the house.

"I am on welfare now. I hate being alive. Why didn't my father let me die? The people are prejudiced here. If you came they would be cruel to us but maybe it would help them see something. You are more beautiful than ever. You are so sexy you make me ache—it is not only because you are black that would be racism but because when you are in the same room with me the room is full of color and scents and I am all alive."

He offered to adopt my daughter, shortly after he received a divorce from his wife.

After my husband and I were divorced (some seven years after Laurel's visit and thirteen years after Laurel and I met), we sat one evening discussing Laurel. He recalled him perfectly, with characteristic empathy and concern.

"If I hadn't been married to you, I would have gone off with him," I said, "Maybe."

"Really?" He seemed surprised.

Out of habit I touched his arm. "I loved him, in a way."

"I know," he said, and smiled.

"A lot of the love was lust. That threw me off for years until I realized lust can be a kind of love."

He nodded.

"I felt guilty about Laurel. When he wrote me, I became anxious. When he came to visit us, I was afraid."

"He was not the man you knew."

"I don't think I knew him well enough to tell. Even so, I was afraid the love and lust would come flying back, along with the pity. And that even if they didn't come back, I would run off with him anyway, because of the pity—*and for the adventure*."

It was the word "adventure" and the different meaning it had for each of us that finally separated us. We had come to understand that, and to accept it without bitterness.

"I wanted to ask you to let me go away with him, for just a couple of months," I said. *"To let me go . . ."*

"He grew steadily worse, you know. His last letters were brutal. He blamed you for everything, even the accident, accusing you of awful, nasty things. He became a bitter, vindictive man."

He knew me well enough to know I heard this and I did not hear it.

He sighed. "It would have been tough for me," he said. "Tough for our daughter. Tough for you. Toughest of all for Laurel."

("Tell me it's all right that I didn't go!" I wanted to plead, but didn't.)

"Right," I said instead, shrugging, and turning our talk to something else.

A LETTER
OF THE TIMES,
OR
SHOULD
THIS
SADO-MASOCHISM
BE SAVED?

Dear Lucy,

You ask why I snubbed you at the Women for Elected Officials Ball. I don't blame you for feeling surprised and hurt. After all, we planned the ball together, expecting to raise our usual pisspot full of money for a good cause. Such a fine idea, our ball: Come as the feminist you most admire! But I did not know you most admired Scarlett O'Hara and so I was, for a moment, taken aback.

I don't know; maybe I should see that picture again. Sometimes when I see movies that hurt me as a child, the pain is minor; I can laugh at the things that made me sad. My trouble with Scarlett was always the forced buffoonery of Prissy, whose strained, slavish voice, as Miz Scarlett pushed her so masterfully up the stairs, I could never get out of my head.

But there is another reason I could not speak to you at the ball that had nothing to do with what is happening just now between us: this heavy bruised silence, this anger and distrust. The day of the ball was my last class day at the University, and it was a very heavy and discouraging day.

Do you remember the things I told you about the class? Its subject was God. That is, the inner spirit, the inner voice; the human compulsion when deeply distressed to seek healing counsel within ourselves, and the capacity within ourselves both to create this counsel and to receive it.

(It had always amused me that the God who spoke to Harriet Tubman and Sojourner Truth told them exactly what they needed to hear, no less than the God of the Old Testament constantly reassured the ancient Jews.)

Indeed, as I read the narratives of black people who were captured and set to slaving away their lives in America, I saw that this inner spirit, this inner capacity for self-comforting, this ability to locate God within that they expressed, demonstrated something marvelous about human beings. Nature has created us with the capacity to know God, to experience God, just as it has created us with the capacity to know speech. The experience of God, or in any case the possibility of experiencing God, *is innate!*

I suppose this has all been thought before; but it came to me as a revelation after reading how the fifth or sixth black woman, finding herself captured, enslaved, sexually abused, starved, whipped, the mother of children she could not want, lover of children she could not have, crept into the corners of the fields, among the haystacks and the animals, and found within her own heart the only solace and love she was ever to know.

It was as if these women found a twin self who saved them from their abused consciousness and chronic physical loneliness; and that twin self is in all of us, waiting only to be summoned.

To prepare my class to comprehend God in this way, I

119

requested they read narratives of these captured black women and also write narratives themselves, as if they *were* those women, or women like them. At the same time, I asked them to write out their own understanding of what the inner voice, "God," is.

It was an extraordinary class, Lucy! With women of all colors, all ages, all shapes and sizes and all conditions. There were lesbians, straights, curveds, celibates, prostitutes, mothers, confuseds, and sundry brilliants of all persuasions! A wonderful class! And almost all of them, though hesitant to admit it at first—who dares talk seriously of "religious" matters these days?—immediately sensed what I meant when I spoke of the inner, companion spirit, of "God."

But what does my class on God have to do with why I snubbed you at the ball? I can hear you wondering. And I will get on to the point.

Lucy, I wanted to teach my students what it felt like to be captured and enslaved. I wanted them to be unable, when they left my class, to think of enslaved women as exotic, picturesque, removed from themselves, deserving of enslavement. I wanted them to be able to repudiate all the racist stereotypes about black women who were enslaved: that they were content, that they somehow "chose" their servitude, that they did not resist.

And so we struggled through an entire semester, during each week of which a student was required to imagine herself a "slave," a mistress or a master, and to come to terms, in imagination and feeling, with what that meant.

Some black women found it extremely difficult to write as captured and enslaved women. (I do not use the word "slaves" casually, because I see enslavement from the enslaved's point of view: there is a world of difference between being a slave and being enslaved). They chose to write as mistress or master. Some white women found it nearly impossible to write as mistress or master, and presumptuous to write as enslaved. Still, there were many fine papers written, Lucy, though there was also much hair tugging and gnashing of teeth.

Black and white and mixed women wrote of captivity, of rape, of forced breeding to restock the master's slave pens. They wrote of attempts to escape, of the sale of their children, of dreams of Africa, of efforts at suicide. No one wrote of acquiescence or of happiness, though one or two, mindful of the religious spirit often infusing the narratives studied, described spiritual ecstasy and joy.

Does anyone want to be a slave? we pondered.

As a class, we thought not.

Imagine our surprise, therefore, when many of us watched a television special on sado-masochism that aired the night before our class ended, and the only interracial couple in it, lesbians, presented themselves as mistress and slave. The white woman, who did all the talking, was mistress (wearing a ring in the shape of a key that she said fit the lock on the chain around the black woman's neck), and the black woman, who stood smiling and silent, was— the white woman said—her slave.

And this is why, though we have been friends for over a decade, Lucy, I snubbed you at the ball.

All I had been teaching was subverted by that one image, and I was incensed to think of the hard struggle of my students to rid themselves of stereotype, to combat prejudice, to put themselves into enslaved women's skins, and then to see their struggle mocked, and the actual enslaved *condition* of literally millions of our mothers trivialized— because two ignorant women insisted on their right to act out publicly a "fantasy" that still strikes terror in black women's hearts. And embarrassment and disgust, at least in the hearts of most of the white women in my class.

One white woman student, apparently with close ties to our local lesbian S&M group, said she could see nothing wrong with what we'd seen on TV. (Incidentally, there

121

were several white men on this program who owned white women as "slaves," and even claimed to hold legal documents to this effect. Indeed, one man paraded his slave around town with a horse's bit between her teeth, and "lent" her out to other sado-masochists to be whipped.) It is all fantasy, she said. No harm done. Slavery, real slavery, is over, after all.

But it isn't over, Lucy, and Kathleen Barry's book on female sexual slavery and Linda Lovelace's book on *being* such a slave are not the only recent indications that this is true. There are places in the world, Lucy, where human beings are still being bought and sold! And so, for that reason, when I saw you at the ball, all I could think was that you were insultingly dressed. No, that is not all I thought: once seeing you dressed as Scarlett, I could not see you. I did not *dare* see you. When you accuse me of looking through you, you are correct. For if I had seen you, Lucy, I'm sure I would have struck you, and with your love of fighting this would surely have meant the end of our ball. And so it was better *not* to see you, to look instead at the woman next to you who had kinked her hair to look like Colette.

A black student said to the S&M sympathizer: I feel abused. I feel my privacy as a black woman has been invaded. Whoever saw that television program can now look at me standing on the corner waiting for a bus and not see *me* at all, but see instead a slave, a creature who *would* wear a chain and lock around my neck for a white person —in 1980!—and accept it. *Enjoy* it.

Her voice shook with anger and hurt.

And so, Lucy, you and I will be friends again because I will talk you out of caring about heroines whose real source of power, as well as the literal shape and condition of their bodies, comes from the people they oppress. But what of the future? What of the women who will never come together because of what they saw in the relationship between "mistress" and "slave" on TV? Many black women fear it is as slaves white women want them; no doubt many white women think some amount of servitude from black women is their due.

But, Lucy, regardless of the "slave" on television, black women do not want to be slaves. They never wanted to be slaves. We will be ourselves and free, or die in the attempt. Harriet Tubman was not our great-grandmother for nothing; which I would advise all black and white women aggressing against us as "mistress" and "slave" to remember. We understand when an attempt is being made to lead us into captivity, though television is a lot more subtle than slave ships. We will simply resist, as we have always done, with ever more accurate weapons of defense.

As a matter of fact, Lucy, it occurs to me that we might plan another ball in the spring as a benefit for this new resistance. What do you think? Do let us get together to discuss it, during the week.

Your friend,
Susan Marie

A
SUDDEN
TRIP
HOME
IN THE
SPRING

For the Wellesley Class

Sarah walked slowly off the tennis court, fingering the back of her head, feeling the sturdy dark hair that grew there. She was popular. As she walked along the path toward Talfinger Hall her friends fell into place around her. They formed a warm jostling group of six. Sarah, because she was taller than the rest, saw the messenger first.

"Miss Davis," he said, standing still until the group came abreast of him, "I've got a telegram for ye." Brian was Irish and always quite respectful. He stood with his cap in his hand until Sarah took the telegram. Then he gave a nod that included all the young ladies before he turned away. He was young and good-looking, though annoyingly servile, and Sarah's friends twittered.

124

"Well, open it!" someone cried, for Sarah stood staring at the yellow envelope, turning it over and over in her hand.

"Look at her," said one of the girls, "isn't she beautiful! Such eyes, and hair, and *skin!*"

Sarah's tall, caplike hair framed a face of soft brown angles, high cheekbones and large dark eyes. Her eyes enchanted her friends because they always seemed to know more, and to find more of life amusing, or sad, than Sarah cared to tell.

Her friends often teased Sarah about her beauty; they loved dragging her out of her room so that their boyfriends, naive and worldly young men from Princeton and Yale, could see her. They never guessed she found this distasteful. She was gentle with her friends, and her outrage at their tactlessness did not show. She was most often inclined to pity them, though embarrassment sometimes drove her to fraudulent expressions. Now she smiled and raised eyes and arms to heaven. She acknowledged their unearned curiosity as a mother endures the prying impatience of a child. Her friends beamed love and envy upon her as she tore open the telegram.

"He's dead," she said.

Her friends reached out for the telegram, their eyes on Sarah.

"It's her father," one of them said softly. "He died yesterday. Oh, Sarah," the girl whimpered, "I'm so sorry!"

"Me too." "So am I." "Is there anything we can do?"

But Sarah had walked away, head high and neck stiff.

"So graceful!" one of her friends said.

"Like a proud gazelle" said another. Then they all trooped to their dormitories to change for supper.

Talfinger Hall was a pleasant dorm. The common room just off the entrance had been made into a small modern art gallery with some very good original paintings, lithographs and collages. Pieces were constantly being stolen.

Some of the girls could not resist an honest-to-God Chagall, signed (in the plate) by his own hand, though they could have afforded to purchase one from the gallery in town. Sarah Davis's room was next door to the gallery, but her walls were covered with inexpensive Gauguin reproductions, a Rubens ("The Head of a Negro"), a Modigliani and a Picasso. There was a full wall of her own drawings, all of black women. She found black men impossible to draw or to paint; she could not bear to trace defeat onto blank pages. Her women figures were matronly, massive of arm, with a weary victory showing in their eyes. Surrounded by Sarah's drawings was a red SNCC poster of a man holding a small girl whose face nestled in his shoulder. Sarah often felt she was the little girl whose face no one could see.

To leave Talfinger even for a few days filled Sarah with fear. Talfinger was her home now; it suited her better than any home she'd ever known. Perhaps she loved it because in winter there was a fragrant fireplace and snow outside her window. When hadn't she dreamed of fireplaces that really warmed, snow that almost pleasantly froze? Georgia seemed far away as she packed; she did not want to leave New York, where, her grandfather had liked to say, "the devil hung out and caught young gals by the front of their dresses." He had always believed the South the best place to live on earth (never mind that certain people invariably marred the landscape), and swore he expected to die no more than a few miles from where he had been born. There was tenacity even in the gray frame house he lived in, and in scrawny animals on his farm who regularly reproduced. He was the first person Sarah wanted to see when she got home.

There was a knock on the door of the adjoining bathroom, and Sarah's suite mate entered, a loud Bach concerto just finishing behind her. At first she stuck just her head into the room, but seeing Sarah fully dressed she trudged in and plopped down on the bed. She was a heavy blonde girl with large milk-white legs. Her eyes were small and her neck usually gray with grime.

"My, don't you look gorgeous," she said.

"Ah, Pam," said Sarah, waving her hand in disgust. In Georgia she knew that even to Pam she would be just another ordinarily attractive *colored* girl. In Georgia there were a million girls better looking. Pam wouldn't know that, of course; she'd never been to Georgia; she'd never even seen a black person to speak to, that is, before she met Sarah. One of her first poetic observations about Sarah was that she was "a poppy in a field of winter roses." She had found it weird that Sarah did not own more than one coat.

"Say listen, Sarah," said Pam, "I heard about your father. I'm sorry. I really am."

"Thanks," said Sarah.

"Is there anything we can do? I thought, well, maybe you'd want my father to get somebody to fly you down. He'd go himself but he's taking Mother to Madeira this week. You wouldn't have to worry about trains and things."

Pamela's father was one of the richest men in the world, though no one ever mentioned it. Pam only alluded to it at times of crisis, when a friend might benefit from the use of a private plane, train, or ship; or, if someone wanted to study the characteristics of a totally secluded village, island or mountain, she might offer one of theirs. Sarah could not comprehend such wealth, and was always annoyed because Pam didn't look more like a billionaire's daughter. A billionaire's daughter, Sarah thought, should really be less horsey and brush her teeth more often.

"Gonna tell me what you're brooding about?" asked Pam.

Sarah stood in front of the radiator, her fingers resting on the window seat. Down below girls were coming up the hill from supper.

"I'm thinking," she said, "of the child's duty to his parents after they are dead."

"Is that all?"

"Do you know," asked Sarah, "about Richard Wright and his father?"

Pamela frowned. Sarah looked down at her.

"Oh, I forgot," she said with a sigh, "they don't teach Wright here. The poshest school in the U.S., and the girls come out ignorant." She looked at her watch, saw she had twenty minutes before her train. "Really," she said almost inaudibly, "why Tears Eliot, Ezratic Pound, and even Sara Teacake, and no Wright?" She and Pamela thought e.e. cummings very clever with his perceptive spelling of great literary names.

"Is he a poet then?" asked Pam. She adored poetry, all poetry. Half of America's poetry she had, of course, not read, for the simple reason that she had never heard of it.

"No," said Sarah, "he wasn't a poet." She felt weary. "He was a man who wrote, a man who had trouble with his father." She began to walk about the room, and came to stand below the picture of the old man and the little girl.

"When he was a child," she continued, "his father ran off with another woman, and one day when Richard and his mother went to ask him for money to buy food he laughingly rejected them. Richard, being very young, thought his father Godlike. Big, omnipotent, unpredictable, undependable and cruel. Entirely in control of his universe. Just like a god. But, many years later, after Wright had become a famous writer, he went down to Mississippi to visit his father. He found, instead of God, just an old watery-eyed field hand, bent from plowing, his teeth gone, smelling of manure. Richard realized that the most daring thing his 'God' had done was run off with that other woman."

128

"So?" asked Pam. "What 'duty' did he feel he owed the old man?"

"So," said Sarah, "that's what Wright wondered as he peered into that old shifty-eyed Mississippi Negro face. What was the duty of the son of a destroyed man? The son of a man whose vision had stopped at the edge of fields that weren't even his. Who was Wright without his father? Was he Wright the great writer? Wright the Communist? Wright the French farmer? Wright whose white wife could never accompany him to Mississippi? Was he, in fact, still his father's son? Or was he freed by his father's desertion to be nobody's son, to be his own father? Could he disavow his father and live? And if so, live as what? As whom? And for what purpose?"

"Well," said Pam, swinging her hair over her shoulders and squinting her small eyes, "if his father rejected him I don't see why Wright even bothered to go see him again. From what you've said, Wright earned the freedom to be whoever he wanted to be. To a strong man a father is not essential."

"Maybe not," said Sarah, "but Wright's father was one faulty door in a house of many ancient rooms. Was that one faulty door to shut him off forever from the rest of the house? That was the question. And though he answered this question eloquently in his work, where it really counted, one can only wonder if he was able to answer it satisfactorily—or at all—in his life."

"You're thinking of his father more as a symbol of something, aren't you?" asked Pam.

"I suppose," said Sarah, taking a last look around her room. "I see him as a door that refused to open, a hand that was always closed. A fist."

Pamela walked with her to one of the college limousines, and in a few minutes she was at the station. The train to the city was just arriving.

———

"Have a nice trip," said the middle-aged driver courteously, as she took her suitcase from him. But for about the thousandth time since she'd seen him, he winked at her.

Once away from her friends she did not miss them. The school was all they had in common. How could they ever know her if they were not allowed to know Wright, she wondered. She was interesting, "beautiful," only because they had no idea what made her, charming only because they had no idea from where she came. And where they came from, though she glimpsed it—in themselves and in F. Scott Fitzgerald—she was never to enter. She hadn't the inclination or the proper ticket.

2

Her father's body was in Sarah's old room. The bed had been taken down to make room for the flowers and chairs and casket. Sarah looked for a long time into the face, as if to find some answer to her questions written there. It was the same face, a dark Shakespearean head framed by gray, woolly hair and split almost in half by a short, gray mustache. It was a completely silent face, a shut face. But her father's face also looked fat, stuffed, and ready to burst. He wore a navy-blue suit, white shirt and black tie. Sarah bent and loosened the tie. Tears started behind her shoulder blades but did not reach her eyes.

"There's a rat here under the casket," she called to her brother, who apparently did not hear her, for he did not come in. She was alone with her father, as she had rarely been when he was alive. When he was alive she had avoided him.

"Where's that girl at?" her father would ask. "Done closed herself up in her room again," he would answer himself.

For Sarah's mother had died in her sleep one night.

Just gone to bed tired and never got up. And Sarah had blamed her father.

Stare the rat down, thought Sarah, surely that will help. *Perhaps it doesn't matter whether I misunderstood or never understood.*

"We moved so much looking for crops, a place to *live*," her father had moaned, accompanied by Sarah's stony silence. "The moving killed her. And now we have a real house, with *four* rooms, and a mailbox on the *porch*, and it's too late. She gone. *She* ain't here to see it." On very bad days her father would not eat at all. At night he did not sleep.

Whatever had made her think she knew what love was or was not?

Here she was, Sarah Davis, immersed in Camusian philosophy, versed in many languages, a poppy, of all things, among winter roses. But before she became a poppy she was a native Georgian sunflower, but still had not spoken the language they both knew. Not to him.

Stare the rat down, she thought, and did. The rascal dropped his bold eyes and slunk away. Sarah felt she had, at least, accomplished something.

Why did she have to see the picture of her mother, the one on the mantel among all the religious doodads, come to life? Her mother had stood stout against the years, clean gray braids shining across the top of her head, her eyes snapping, protective. Talking to her father.

"He called you out your name, we'll leave this place today. Not tomorrow. That be too late. Today!" Her mother was magnificent in her quick decisions.

"But what about your garden, the children, the change of schools?" Her father would be holding, most likely, the wide brim of his hat in nervously twisting fingers.

"He called you out your name, we go!"

And go they would. Who knew exactly where, before they moved? Another soundless place, walls falling down, roofing gone; another face to please without leaving too much of her father's pride at his feet. But to Sarah then, no matter with what alacrity her father moved, foot-dragging alone was visible.

The moving killed her, her father had said, *but the moving was also love.*

Did it matter now that often he had threatened their lives with the rage of his despair? That once he had spanked the crying baby violently, who later died of something else altogether . . . and that the next day they moved?

"No," said Sarah aloud, "I don't think it does."

"Huh?" It was her brother, tall, wiry, black, deceptively calm. As a child he'd had an irrespressible temper. As a grown man he was tensely smooth, like a river that any day will overflow its bed.

He had chosen a dull gray casket. Sarah wished for red. Was it Dylan Thomas who had said something grand about the dead offering "deep, dark defiance"? It didn't matter; there were more ways to offer defiance than with a red casket.

"I was just thinking," said Sarah, "that with us Mama and Daddy were saying NO with capital letters."

"I don't follow you," said her brother. He had always been the activist in the family. He simply directed his calm rage against any obstacle that might exist, and awaited the consequences with the same serenity he awaited his sister's answer. Not for him the philosophical confusions and poetic observations that hung his sister up.

"That's because you're a radical preacher," said Sarah, smiling up at him. "You deliver your messages in person with your own body." It excited her that her brother had at last imbued their childhood Sunday sermons with the reality of fighting for change. And saddened her that no matter how she looked at it this seemed more important than Medieval Art, Course 201.

"Yes, Grandma," Sarah replied. "Cresselton is for girls only, and *no*, Grandma, I am not pregnant."

Her grandmother stood clutching the broad wooden handle of her black bag, which she held, with elbows bent, in front of her stomach. Her eyes glinted through round wire-framed glasses. She spat into the grass outside the privy. She had insisted that Sarah accompany her to the toilet while the body was being taken into the church. She had leaned heavily on Sarah's arm, her own arm thin and the flesh like crepe.

"I guess they teach you how to really handle the world," she said. "And who knows, the Lord is everywhere. I would like a whole lot to see a Great-Grand. You don't specially have to be married, you know. That's why I felt free to ask." She reached into her bag and took out a Three Sixes bottle, which she proceeded to drink from, taking deep swift swallows with her head thrown back.

"There are very few black boys near Cresselton," Sarah explained, watching the corn liquor leave the bottle in spurts and bubbles. "Besides, I'm really caught up now in my painting and sculpting. . . ." Should she mention how much she admired Giacometti's work? No, she decided. Even if her grandmother had heard of him, and Sarah was positive she had not, she would surely think his statues much too thin. This made Sarah smile and remember how difficult it had been to convince her grandmother that even if Cresselton had not given her a scholarship she would have managed to go there anyway. Why? Because she wanted somebody to teach her to paint and to sculpt, and Cresselton had the best teachers. Her grandmother's notion of a successful granddaughter was a married one, pregnant the first year.

"Well," said her grandmother, placing the bottle with

dignity back into her purse and gazing pleadingly into Sarah's face, "I sure would 'preshate a Great-Grand." Seeing her granddaughter's smile, she heaved a great sigh, and, walking rather haughtily over the stones and grass, made her way to the church steps.

As they walked down the aisle, Sarah's eyes rested on the back of her grandfather's head. He was sitting on the front middle bench in front of the casket, his hair extravagantly long and white and softly kinked. When she sat down beside him, her grandmother sitting next to him on the other side, he turned toward her and gently took her hand in his. Sarah briefly leaned her cheek against his shoulder and felt like a child again.

4

They had come twenty miles from town, on a dirt road, and the hot spring sun had drawn a steady rich scent from the honeysuckle vines along the way. The church was a bare, weather-beaten ghost of a building with hollow windows and a sagging door. Arsonists had once burned it to the ground, lighting the dry wood of the walls with the flames from the crosses they carried. The tall spreading red oak tree under which Sarah had played as a child still dominated the churchyard, stretching its branches widely from the roof of the church to the other side of the road.

After a short and eminently dignified service, during which Sarah and her grandfather alone did not cry, her father's casket was slid into the waiting hearse and taken the short distance to the cemetery, an overgrown wilderness whose stark white stones appeared to be the small ruins of an ancient civilization. There Sarah watched her grandfather from the corner of her eye. He did not seem to bend under the grief of burying a son. His back was straight, his eyes dry and clear. He was simply and solemnly heroic; a man who kept with pride his family's trust and his own grief. *It is strange,* Sarah thought, *that I never thought to paint him like this, simply as he stands; without anonymous meaningless people hovering beyond his profile; his face turned proud and brownly against the light.* The defeat that had frightened her in the faces of black men was the defeat of black forever defined by white. But that defeat was nowhere on her grandfather's face. He stood like a rock, outwardly calm, the comfort and support of the Davis family. The family alone defined him, and he was not about to let them down.

"One day I will paint you, Grandpa," she said, as they turned to go. "Just as you stand here now, with just"— she moved closer and touched his face with her hand— "just the right stubborn tenseness of your cheek. Just that look of Yes and No in your eyes."

"You wouldn't want to paint an old man like me," he said, looking deep into her eyes from wherever his mind had been. "If you want to make me, make me up in stone."

The completed grave was plump and red. The wreaths of flowers were arranged all on one side so that from the road there appeared to be only a large mass of flowers. But already the wind was tugging at the rose petals and the rain was making dabs of faded color all over the green foam frames. In a week the displaced honeysuckle vines, the wild roses, the grapevines, the grass, would be back. Nothing would seem to have changed.

5

"What do you mean, come *home?*" Her brother seemed genuinely amused. "We're all proud of you. How many black girls are at that school? Just *you?* Well, just one more besides you, and she's from the North. That's really something!"

"I'm glad you're pleased," said Sarah.

"Pleased! Why, it's what Mama would have wanted, a good education for little Sarah; and what Dad would have wanted too, if he could have wanted anything after Mama died. You were always smart. When you were two and I was five you showed me how to eat ice cream without getting it all over me. First, you said, nip off the bottom of the cone with your teeth, and suck the ice cream down. I never knew *how* you were supposed to eat the stuff once it began to melt."

"I don't know," she said, "sometimes you can want something a whole lot, only to find out later that it wasn't what you *needed* at all."

Sarah shook her head, a frown coming between her eyes. "I sometimes spend *weeks*," she said, "trying to sketch or paint a face that is unlike every other face around me, except, vaguely, for one. Can I help but wonder if I'm in the right place?"

Her brother smiled. "You mean to tell me you spend *weeks* trying to draw one face, and you still wonder whether you're in the right place? You must be kidding!" He chucked her under the chin and laughed out loud. "You learn how to draw the face," he said, "then you learn how to paint me and how to make Grandpa up in stone. Then you can come home or go live in Paris, France. It'll be the same thing."

It was the unpreacherlike gaiety of his affection that made her cry. She leaned peacefully into her brother's arms. She wondered if Richard Wright had had a brother.

"You are my door to all the rooms," she said. "Don't ever close."

And he said, "I won't," as if he understood what she meant.

6

"When will we see you again, young woman?" he asked later, as he drove her to the bus stop.

"I'll sneak up one day and surprise you," she said.

At the bus stop, in front of a tiny service station, Sarah hugged her brother with all her strength. The white station attendant stopped his work to leer at them, his eyes bold and careless.

"Did you ever think," said Sarah, "that we are a very old people in a very young place?"

She watched her brother from a window of the bus; her eyes did not leave his face until the little station was out of sight and the big Greyhound lurched on its way toward Atlanta. She would fly from there to New York.

7

She took the train to the campus.

"My," said one of her friends, "you look wonderful! Home sure must agree with you!"

"Sarah was home?" Someone who didn't know asked. "Oh, *great*, how was it?"

"Well, how was it?" went an echo in Sarah's head. The noise of the echo almost made her dizzy.

"How was it?" she asked aloud, searching for, and regaining, her balance.

"How was it?" She watched her reflection in a pair of smiling hazel eyes.

"It was fine," she said slowly, returning the smile, thinking of her grandfather. "Just fine."

The girl's smile deepened. Sarah watched her swinging along toward the back tennis courts, hair blowing in the wind.

Stare the rat down, thought Sarah; *and whether it disappears or not, I am a woman in the world. I have buried my father, and shall soon know how to make my grandpa up in stone.*

SOURCE

It was during the year of her first depressing brush with government funding of antipoverty programs that San Francisco began to haunt Irene. An educational project into which she'd poured much of her time, energy and considerable talent was declared "superfluous and romantic" by Washington, and summarily killed; Irene began to long for every amenity the small, dusty Southern town she worked in did not offer. With several other young, idealistic people, she had taught "Advanced Reading and Writing" to a small group of older women. Their entire "school" was a secondhand trailer in back of a local black college; the books they used were written by the teachers and students themselves. The women had a desire for learning that was exciting; the town, however, was dull; its main attraction a grimy, only recently desegregated movie theater with an abandoned appreciation for Burt

Reynolds. Irene daydreamed incessantly of hilly streets, cable cars, Chinatown and Rice-o-Roni. Of redwood forests and the Pacific Ocean.

She decided to visit a friend from her New York college days, Anastasia Green. Anastasia now lived in San Francisco, and frequently wrote, inviting her to visit, should she ever make it to that fabled city.

Anastasia was tall and willowy, with cautious, smoky topaz eyes, hair the color of unpolished brass, and a mouth that seemed much smaller than her teeth, so that when she smiled the planes of her face shifted radically to accommodate a sudden angularity in a face that had seemed round. This irregularity in her features was not grotesque, but charming, and gave to Anastasia's face a humor she herself did not possess.

While Irene knew her on the East Coast, Anastasia went through two complete external changes: The first was from the "Southern Innocent" (she was from Pine Lake, Arkansas), wide-eyed, blushing, absurdly trusting—but not really —to the New York SuperVamp. Tall boots, of course, slickly bobbed *blackened* hair, heavily made-up eyes (brown and black make-up, a rather Egyptian effect), against skin that by contrast seemed to have been dusted with rice powder, and, in fact, had been. The second change was to a sort of Faye Dunaway, whom she—with her peculiar smile—somewhat resembled, or what she referred to as her "little English schoolboy look." Hair lightened and cropped close to her (it was now revealed) *round* little head, bangs down to her eyebrows, skirts up to her ass. And always a swinging purse and absurd snub-toed shoes. In this getup she didn't walk, she *tripped* along, and one was not surprised if, when she passed trippingly by, "Eleanor Rigby" popped into mind.

It was while in this disguise that she fell in love with a man named Galen, who was as addicted to the theater as Anastasia was to travel. After college, Galen left the East

Coast for the West, where he hoped to become an actor. He convinced Anastasia to come along. From letters, Irene knew that Galen had dropped out of the picture, so to speak, while doing TV commercials in Los Angeles. Anastasia, already rinsing her hair in vinegar and staying out in the sun, had pressed north.

TV documentaries about the flower children of the sixties carried many shots of people who looked like Anastasia–in–San Francisco. Gone was the vamp, the English schoolboy. Instead, she appeared in clogs, a long granny dress of an old-fashioned print and sleazy texture, with a purple velvet cape. The kinkiness of her hair was now encouraged, and formed an aura about her beige, unpowdered face. She was beaded and feathered to a delightfully pleasant extreme.

"It's great to see you!" the two women said almost in unison, embracing and smiling, amid the anxious and harried looking travelers at the airport.

With Anastasia were a young man, a young woman, and their baby. The baby's name was very long, Sanskrit-derived, and, translated into English, meant Bliss. The man's name, arrived at in the same fashion, meant Calm, and the woman's name, Peace. All three adults giggled easily and at everything, absent-mindedly fingering small silver spoons that hung around their necks.

Not knowing what the spoon signified, Irene was amused by it. Unisex jewelry, she thought, had finally hit the mark.

There was a van, painted all the colors of the rainbow, so that simply riding along felt *vivid*. The adults were soon chanting and singing; the baby was kicking and cooing. They crossed merrily over the bridge into Marin, to which Anastasia and her friends had recently moved. From there they would "strike" day trips into San Francisco.

"Source would love Irene," said Peace or Calm.

"He sure would!" Anastasia agreed, turning to give

140

Irene's arm a squeeze. "I've told them you're one of the least rigid people I know."

Happy as Irene was whenever there were strange creatures to observe or meet, she did not hesitate—silently, of course—to agree. Who would *not* love me? was her attitude. The trauma of having lost the educational project had not damaged an essential self-saving vanity.

"Who is 'Source'?" Irene asked languidly, because by now the van was filled with mellow *sinsamilla* smoke.

"Wait and see," said Anastasia, mysteriously.

They lived in a large, rambling house on a hillside in Marin. The rooms were light and airy and filled with sunshine, Indian prints, seashells, rocks, paper mobiles, and lacy straw mats. From every window there was a view: the bay, sailboats; Tiburon, across the Bay.

"How do you manage all this?" Irene asked, glancing in a cupboard stacked high with bags of granola.

"Food stamps and relief," said Anastasia, with a slight shrug. It was the kind of shrug Irene was seeing a lot. There was . . . dissatisfaction in it; there was also acceptance. Missing—and, suddenly, it seemed to Irene—was defiance.

Bliss and her parents, Calm and Peace, disappeared into a separate part of the house. Anastasia and Irene sat down at the kitchen table.

"In parts of the country," Irene said in a voice modulated to show this meant nothing whatsoever to her, "the amount of assistance people get is less, by design, than they can live on."

Anastasia leaned forward, and in an equally nonpartisan tone, said, "It is *much* better to be on welfare in a rich place than in a poor one. Not only do rich people here dress the way we do—if anything they're more tattered and less stylish—but they are *so* rich it delights them to support us in our poverty."

Irene laughed, dutifully.

"How is your teaching?" asked Anastasia. Like many of Irene's friends, she never read the newsletter that Irene and her group published, in which they discussed in detail methods of teaching older people, under- and miseducated young people, or what they called among themselves, just as society did, "the Unteachables." Only they said it with an informed sense of humor, not yet having encountered an absolute "unteachable."

For a moment, Irene debated with herself whether to respond with more than "okay." In stories, in literature, such work as she did sounds romantic, as well as idealistic. The reality, day to day, is different. In Irene's case there was, first of all, the incredible brain-broiling heat of the Southern summer, when the majority of her students—all women in their late forties, fifties and sixties—could attend classes from one to three weeks at a time. The trailer they used was not air-conditioned, and there were flies. Sometimes classes were crowded, and composed of people who—from years of being passive spectators in church, required only to respond in shouts or "amens"—found it difficult to take an active part in their own instruction. They doubted their own personal histories and their own experience. The food—donated by the local college whose backyard they were in—was bad. Bologna and pork and beans and yellow, wilted slices of lettuce. Oversweetened lemonade that attracted mosquitoes. And there was the smell of clean poverty, an odor Irene wished would disappear from the world, a sharp, *bitter* odor, almost acrid, as if the women washed themselves in chemicals.

Teaching was exciting only sporadically, when student or teacher learned something. Often no one seemed to learn anything. In desperation Irene would sometimes show films, because whatever the films were about, they seemed to threaten her students less than Irene's constant insistence that they acknowledge their own oppression, as

142

blacks *and* as women. From films like "Birth of a Nation" there would be an immediate rise; from a film like "Anna Lucasta" a stunned and bewildered silence. At first, anyway.

"It's not going well," Irene said, as Anastasia put a filter into the Chemex, spooned in coffee, and poured on boiling water. Through the low-slung kitchen window Irene saw the fog sliding into the garden, a cat napping on a rock, and a round terra-cotta urn of herbs on the back steps. There was a peace and unreality about the house.

"You wrote me about your school," Anastasia said as noncommittally as possible, as they sipped mellow black coffee and munched on homemade carrot cake.

There was a side of Irene that Anastasia did not like. It was the side that seemed unnecessarily obsessed with the dark, seedy side of life. They'd once discussed Anastasia's inability to get involved in projects that interested Irene, and Anastasia had shrugged and said, "You're into pain!" They had laughed, but Anastasia realized Irene thought her incapable of deep emotion, and so, in a way, talked (or wrote) down to her. Since this spared her a lot of *Sturm und Drang*, she thought this was okay, and didn't complain. She accepted the shallowness this attitude assured.

It didn't occur to Irene that Anastasia could empathize with her commitments, and their college friendship had been based largely on a shared love of movies and jazz. Though she feigned a good-humored acceptance of Anastasia's easygoing life style, and her reliance on personal fashion to indicate the state of her mind, on a deeper level, she felt contempt for her, as a person who chose to be of limited use.

"It ended for lack of funds," Irene said.

"Who funded it?" asked Anastasia, politely.

Irene sighed, and began in a rush. "In the beginning, there *was* no funding." The two women could not help grinning in recognition of the somehow *familiar* sound of this: they had both been brought up in the church. "In the beginning, there *was* no funding," repeated Irene. "The women wanted to learn before they 'got too old' and they simply talked—and in some cases shamed— younger women into teaching them. Then there was a grant from the government that paid those like me who came from outside. The trouble with government funding, of course, is that it is so fucking fickle. . . . With the war going on in Vietnam, and bombs to be bought, government could hardly be expected to care that a few dozen *old* black women still believe in education."

"I thought you said in your letters that some of the women are white," said Anastasia, resting her chin on the back of her hand, and gazing steadily at Irene. She liked to look at Irene, liked her sometimes *fierce* brown eyes, liked very much the dark richness of her skin—but she could never say so.

"Oh yes," said Irene, "some of them are. Three, in fact." When white people reached a certain level of poverty (assuming they were not members of the Klan, or worse, which they very often were), they ceased to be "white" to her. Like many of her quasi-political beliefs, however, she had not thought this through. She was afraid to, and this was one of the major failings in her character. If she thought this through, for example, she would have to think of what becomes of poor whites when (if) they become rich (and how could she waste her time teaching incipient rich, white people?) and what becomes of blacks when they become middle class; she was already contemptuous of the black middle class. In fact, for its boringly slavish imitation of the white middle class, which she considered mediocre in its tiniest manifestations, she hated it. And yet, technically, she was now a part of this class.

If she began questioning these things, she would have to

question her own place in society and how she was going to
be a success at whatever she did (she had few doubts about
her capabilities and none about her energy) but at the same
time avoid becoming bourgeois. She enjoyed so many bourgeois pleasures, and yet she loathed the thought of settling
for them. Just as jazz was her favorite music because it held
the middle class in abeyance, *Steppenwolf* was the novel
that, since college, had most enduringly reflected her mind.

"Can the women go back to learning the way they did
before the funding?" asked Anastasia.

"One day they might," said Irene. "I don't know. A
funny thing happened to them, and to me, around the
funding from government. At first it lifted our spirits,
made us believe someone up there in D.C. cared about the
lives of these women, the deliberate impoverishment of
their particular past. And the women settled down to learn
in that belief. As amazingly as the funding began, though,
it ended. We had just had time to get used to more than
we had before when suddenly there was nothing at all.
We had 'progressed' to a new level only to find ourselves
stranded. To go back to the old way would feel like
defeat."

As Irene talked, she thought of one of the women in her
class who particularly moved her, and who resisted learning to read because everything she was required to read
was so painful. Irene had had to coax her back to class
after the first day. On the first day, the woman, whose name
was Fania, had expressed a strong desire to learn to read.
She was a stout, walnut-colored woman who wore her hair
in braids that crossed at the back of her neck and, in her
ears, small gold loops. Her embarrassment at not knowing
how to read was so acute that, in admitting it, she kept her
eyes tightly shut, and in the course of making a very short
statement of her condition, she undid both braids and
managed to get the earrings tangled in her hair.

Like so much that is deeply tragic, this sight was also

comic. Realizing how she must appear to the class, and to Irene, Fania had blushed darkly and offered a short puzzled laugh at herself. It was a look and a laugh that Irene never forgot.

Irene had had much success teaching reading by using the newspapers. She found nonreaders related quickly to news about what was going on in their midst, and that often too they recognized certain words—like names of towns, stores, and so on—with which they were already familiar. Each time they "read" a word they already knew, they were encouraged.

For Fania, Irene had chosen a rather innocuous item about the increasing mechanization of farm labor, which was the kind of work most of her students knew well. She thought the words "fertilizer distributor," "automatic weeder," "cotton picker" and the like would be easy. They were long words, true, but words used every day by the women, as they passed by plantations where this new machinery was already in operation.

Irene read quickly over the short news item, to rob it of any surprise. Surprises in any form, she had discovered, inhibited these would-be readers.

" 'Way, Georgia: Sources at the Department of Agriculture predict that in less than ten years, farming as our state has known it for generations will no longer exist. Widespread use of fertilizer distributors, automatic weeders and cotton pickers will virtually wipe out the need for human labor. Thousands of tenant farmers who have traditionally farmed the land, have already been displaced. Crop prices —including those for soybeans and peanuts—are expected to continue to rise. It is expected that automation will increase profits and stimulate the growth of other industries that are beginning to relocate in the South because of the abundance of energy, in terms of both the environment and the ever-populous, non-unionized, labor pool.' "

Fania had stammered, choked, pulled at her earrings

146

and her braids—but in the end had simply refused to learn to read that the only work she'd ever known would soon not exist.

While Irene talked, Anastasia fingered the colorful straw place mat in front of her. As so often happened when she talked to another black person, the world seemed weighted down with problems. "You can't improve anything, you know?" she said. "You can't change anything. I've learned that from Source."

Irene waited. Anastasia seemed inspired.

"Source got me and my folks together again. You won't believe this, but we write to each other now at least once a week. Hey, let me show you . . ." Anastasia rose and disappeared into another room. She returned with a bundle of letters. She peeled off a letter from the bundle and spread the pages on the table. She changed her mind about reading aloud to Irene, who was looking at her, she felt, skeptically. She pushed the letter toward Irene, who glanced quickly over it.

Anastasia's parents had once been Baptists; they were now Jehovah's Witnesses. There was a lot in the letter about continuing to love her and even more about continuing to petition Jehovah God in her behalf. From the letter, prayers were going up from Arkansas by the hour. The hair rose at the back of Irene's neck, but she forced herself to remain calm.

Irene had met Anastasia's family once, by design, she always thought, on Anastasia's part. Irene lived for a time in a terrible D.C. slum, and represented, therefore, a kind of educated lunatic fringe to those friends who thought poverty in and of itself was dangerous to visitors. While her parents were in town, Anastasia asked to stay with Irene, though in fact she was at that time living with her friend Galen. Her parents had driven up in the longest pink Lincoln Continental Irene had ever seen. Her father and brothers had braved the trashy street to come up to

Irene's flat, but her mother had waited in the car—doors locked and windows rolled up tight—until Anastasia and Irene were brought out to her. Her gray, stricken eyes clutched at Irene's. Why? Why? they asked, while her mouth said how pleased she was they had finally met. "What is she afraid of?" Irene had asked Anastasia; "What *isn't* she afraid of?" Anastasia had replied.

Anastasia's brothers were amber-skinned and curly-haired, with the slouching posture and menacing non-language of other boys their age. They were fifteen and sixteen. Anastasia's father was an olive-skinned, crinkly-haired man whose intense inner turmoil and heaviness of spirit caused an instant recoiling; on his face, one felt a smile would look unnatural.

This father now wrote of God's love, God's grace, God's assured forgiveness, and of his own happiness that his daughter, always, at heart, "a *good* girl," had at last embarked on *the path of obedience*. This path alone led to peace everlasting, in the new and coming system of the world.

"*Obedience*," thought Irene. "*Peace Everlasting*! Holy shit!"

"I wanted to do good, too," said Anastasia, and laughed. "Of course all the 'doing good' is really for yourself, nobody else. Nobody ever does anybody else any good. The good they do is for them. Altruism doesn't exist. Neither do good works."

"Wait a minute," said Irene, a clenched fist resting on the letters in her lap. "I believe in movements, collective action to influence the future, and all that. Basically, I believe somebody is responsible for the child."

"People should understand," said Anastasia, speaking very fast and somewhat blindly, Irene felt, as if she were speaking with her eyes closed, so that for a moment she reminded Irene of Fania, "that when they suffer it is because they *choose* suffering. If you suffer in a place, leave."

The baby was awake now and Irene was holding him. His thick hair smelled of incense. His slender fingers probed her nose.

"You can't leave a baby," Irene said.

"Men do it all the time."

"Women stay because they don't want to be 'men.' "

"And men go because they don't want to be women— that half of the human race that never realizes it has a choice."

"But who will look after the children?"

"Someone will," she said, "or won't." She looked into Irene's face.

"It's all the same." She shrugged. "That's the point."

The baby's mother came into the room. She had a face the color of a pink towel, a stout figure and blue eyes shaped like arrows. Spiritual striving was most apparent in her speech; over her harsh New York accent she'd poured a sweetness that hurt the ears.

"It's a beautiful baby," Irene said, as she plucked grapes off a bunch on the table and began plopping them into her own and the baby's mouths.

"Thank you," she cooed. "We're giving him to Anastasia. She loves him so much and is such a good mommy. We're going to South America."

"When?" asked Irene.

She shrugged. "Sometime."

"Was that hard to decide?" Irene wanted to know.

"Source teaches us that all children belong to everyone, to the whole world."

"But not to anyone in particular?"

She sang, "That's right," and swept out of the room.

"We have to take you to meet Source," said Peace, who came in next and rummaged through the grapes. He was emaciated, far taller than the refrigerator and wore his long straw-colored hair in a ponytail tied with a bright green cord. A brilliant red birthmark, shaped like a tiny foot, "walked" across his nose.

Source lived in a large apartment house very close by. One of his daughters, a thin, sad-eyed girl in her teens, her long black hair shining against her sallow brown skin, showed them up to his flat. After admitting them she kept her gaze below their knees.

Anastasia, Peace, Calm and Bliss had brought an offering of wine and money, which they placed on a table near Source's feet. Source himself was seated in the lotus position on a round bed shoved against the wall of the otherwise bare and dingy room. The guests were offered cushions on the floor. A second daughter padded up silently, her eyes as sad as the first's, and poured the wine into glasses which she handed to each of them. She also lit a stick of incense. Soon the room was hazy with smoke and the air heavy with the sweet, oppressive smell.

A third daughter came and stood at her father's left hand, which he periodically raised and sent her scurrying into the other rooms for something he wanted.

"It is possible that all swamis look alike," Irene was thinking. Source was a pale, grayish brown, with dark glittery eyes and graying dark hair parted in the middle and hanging about his shoulders. He wore a white robe that he used, as he talked, to cover and uncover his bare feet. It was a slow, flipping motion that relaxed and in a way hypnotized his audience.

Irene was determined not to think any of the prejudicial things she was thinking, and adjusted her face to show interest, concern, anticipatory delight.

Source's voice had a whine and a drone somewhere in it, however, and this made it objectionable. He was saying how the first time he met Anastasia, whom he called, in Sanskrit, Tranquility, she looked exactly like Kathleen

Cleaver, "dressed all entirely completely in black" (he was to use triple qualifiers frequently). "Her hair like an angry, wild, animal bush. And her skin pale pale pale, like that one. Militant, you see?" He laughed, fluttered the fingers of his left hand in the air beside his nose, and the sad-eyed daughter standing beside him shifted the pillow behind his back.

Anastasia was laughing, fingering her spoon and occasionally sniffling and rubbing her eyes, which were red and glassy.

"Well"—she shrugged—"I thought I was black."

"Nobody's anything," said Source, as to a dense child, and Anastasia shrugged again.

Source called out sharply. There was a flurry of movement in the kitchen, and his other two daughters came and stood next to the one who had remained beside the bed.

"Nobody's anything," he repeated. The daughter began to write down his words. Through her rather bedraggled sari it was clear she was pregnant.

"I used to live in Africa, in Uganda," continued Source, "and the Africans wanted to be black black black. They were always saying it: black black black. But that is because Africans are backward people. You see? Indians do not go about saying, 'We are brown brown brown,' or the Chinese, 'yellow yellow yellow.' "

"No," said Irene, "they say they are Chinese Chinese Chinese and Indian Indian Indian."

However, it was out of line to speak while Source spoke. He continued as if she had not interrupted.

"Africans are strange creatures. I will tell you a story that really happened in Africa. An African . . ."

It was such an ancient racist joke, Irene had not heard it since she was a small child. "The African" in it as stupid, lazy, backward and unmotivated to improve as any colonialist could wish. Tranquility, Peace and Calm and even the baby—whose vicariously stoned response to the world was a look of slack wonder—giggled.

"Where are you going?" asked Tranquility, as Irene rose.

"I'll meet you on the street," Irene said.

On the way back, Peace and Calm talked disjointedly of ego and humility and how they now, since knowing Source, had none of the former and lots of the latter. It was hinted that Irene might likewise be improved.

"Is the pregnant daughter married?" she asked coldly.

"Why should she be?" asked Calm.

"She has Source," sniffed Peace.

Which was precisely what Irene feared, but she decided against pursuing it.

"Who supports Source?" she asked.

"We all do," they said proudly. "Source is too precious to waste his life working."

A moment later, Tranquility said, "He's a teacher, like you. Teaching *is* his work."

"I'm sorry," said Anastasia next day. "But we have decided you have to go."

"What?" asked Irene.

"You disapprove of us."

"I don't understand you."

"Listen," said Anastasia. "I've finally got my life together, and it's all thanks to Source. I understand I am nothing. That is what Source was testing you to see. You still think you are Somebody. That you matter. That Africans matter. They don't," she said. "And if they are nothing—if nobody's anything—it is impossible to humiliate them."

"But he's a racist; he treats his daughters like slaves."

"He is above all that. You *don't* understand. *Right*. But see, if nobody's anything, everyone is equal. That's clear enough, isn't it?"

"Clear enough, but impossible."

"Before I had my breakdown I didn't understand either. I wanted to *be* Kathleen Cleaver. I met her once at a party in New York before *she* was Kathleen Cleaver. She had long straight, light-colored hair, like mine, *just* like mine, and she sat in a corner all evening without saying a word. Not one. Men did all the talking. Months later, she changed. Suddenly she was doing the talking because the men were dead or in jail. She cursed a lot, she dressed in boots and sunglasses and black clothes and posed for photographers holding a gun. I did all that. I even found a revolutionary black man to live with who beat me— and thought nothing of forbidding me to talk to what he considered 'strangers,' even though they were my friends.

"My parents came from Arkansas and got me. They had me locked away in a 'rest' home. It was a long time before I could see their point of view.

"When I was a child I wanted to change things. When the sit-ins started I wanted to join. I wanted to integrate schools and lunch counters. But I was so *fair*, and I'd never even seen my own hair unstraightened; mother started having it straightened when I was three, for God's sake. . . . But my color wasn't the problem. Oh *God*, I'm so *bored* with color being the problem. It was my undeveloped comprehension of the world. My parents already *had* the Truth, which is why they love Source so much, as much as I do. They knew nobody's anything, that color is an illusion, that the universe is unchangeable. Source teaches us nothing can be changed, all suffering is self-indulgence and the good of life is, basically, indifference to it—pleasure, if that is possible."

"The good of life is *indifference?*"

"They released me into Source's care. They help support him, financially. It works out."

The baby, hungry, was crying and crawling over the floor. Irene walked over to him and picked him up. His

153

mother flew into the room and snatched him from her arms.

"We try to protect him from bad vibes," she said.

"*Bitch*," said Irene, under her breath, then she turned again to Anastasia, who was trembling from the righteousness of her stand.

"Anastasia," Irene said, "I didn't come all this way to criticize your life. I came all this way because mine is lying kaput all around me, remember?" She knew she wasn't wrong about Source, but what did he matter? she thought. "Perhaps I was wrong about Source. Perhaps you are right to defend him. This is a bad time in my life to have someone like that sprung on me, actually. I was predisposed not to like him; maybe he sensed this. . . ." She rambled on, but Anastasia was not listening. She imagined Anastasia, Peace and Calm meeting in the dead of night to plan just this scene between them. It seemed to her that only the baby, Bliss, had welcomed her, from the start.

"Your life is what you make it," Anastasia said, stonily.

"But that's *absurd*. Not everyone's life is what they make it. Some people's life is what other people make it. I would say this is true of the majority of the people in the world. The women I teach didn't choose to be illiterate, didn't choose to be poor."

"But *you* chose to teach that kind of people. Why complain?"

"*That* kind of people?"

"Miserable. Hopeless in this incarnation."

Irene laughed. "You make me think of Kissinger, who said, 'This is not Africa's century.' "

Anastasia did not smile.

"I didn't mean to complain," Irene said, humiliated at the thought.

"If you suffer in a place, *leave*," Anastasia said with conviction, and, Irene thought, a great deal of smugness.

"If you suffer in a *condition?*"

Anastasia lifted her spoon.

It was now years later for almost everyone. It was certainly years later for Irene, who was astounded one day to find herself discussing teaching methods with a group of Native American and white women educators in Alaska.

"As soon as I heard you were coming," said Anastasia, who now lived near Anchorage, "I told my man, 'I have to go see her; she's an old friend!' "

They were sitting in a bar that on clear days boasted a perfect view of Mt. McKinley, a hundred miles away. Alas, clear days were apparently rare, and Irene had seen nothing of Alaska's legendary mountains but their feet. But even these were impressive.

"You've forgiven me, I hope, for throwing you out," said Anastasia.

"Oh, sure," said Irene. She was looking at the other people in the bar. She liked Alaska. She liked the way the people looked as if they had come, that very month, from someplace else. The damp weather, however, though not cold—as she had expected it to be—made her long for the sun, for fireplaces, for a less penetrable selection of clothing than she'd brought.

Anastasia had snared her directly from the stage, where Irene had sat beside a Native Alaskan woman who talked of the failing eyesight of Alaskans, who were reading print, over long periods, for the first time.

"Native Alaskans always took perfect vision for granted," the woman had said. "Then comes this reading. This television. This shopping where everything is labeled with words for more reading. Everybody needs glasses now to see anything at all." She was wearing huge aviator glasses with purple lenses. She yanked them off and blinked at the audience. It was a long pause, during which she dropped the assertive stance of her statement and seemed, somewhere inside herself, to fold. "There's a basic distrust maybe," she continued softly, "about acquiring knowledge in a way that can make you blind. This has to be behind many of our older people's reading problems."

Irene didn't doubt it for a moment.

Anastasia had taken Irene's arm and stood close beside her while Native Alaskan educators pressed her hand warmly. "So good to see you!" they said, as if they had been waiting for her. "So happy you could come all this way up from the Lower 48!"

"When I heard you were coming, and that it would be a conference about Natives, I thought I'd be the only white chick around. But I see I'm not."

Irene did not blink at this.

And now they sat at the bar, with its famous absent view of Mt. McKinley. Irene felt drained from the panel discussion. Thinking of the woman in the aviator glasses, she was also depressed. She finished her first Irish whiskey and ordered another. When she looked at Anastasia, whose hair was now in braids and held by leather thongs with feathers, and whose eyes literally danced, it was as if Anastasia were receding, receding, receding, into the blurred landscape. But this was a momentary and maudlin vision, which Irene had another gulp of her drink to squelch.

"So," she said, "nobody's anything."

"I heard you were happily married," said Anastasia, ignoring Irene's remark.

"We *were* happy. I'm almost sure we were happy. You know happiness is being able to assume you are happy. Anyway, he left me."

"I *love* being white," Anastasia said, plunging in and screwing up her face in a mock excess of delight. "Ask me why."

"Why?" said Irene.

"Because as a black person I had no sense of humor!"
She laughed, and her funny face and her laughter meshed.

"I can't deny that," said Irene. "Besides, passing for
white is so—so—*color*ful." She meant, really, that it was
passé.

"No, no," said Anastasia. "That's *Imitation of Life*—
and what was that other tacky movie? *Pinky?* Not even a
Jessie Fauset or a Nella Larsen novel, where being white
is such a to-do about what colors now look good against
your skin. There *were* shades of *Autobiography of an Ex-
Colored Man* in the beginning—you know, could a po-
tentially *great* black woman find happiness as a mediocre
white one?—but that passed." She laughed. "Anyway, I'm
not passing; I'm just through trying to correct other
people's opinion."

Irene, staring directly into Anastasia's eyes, felt the
strangest sensation. Those eyes now looked out of a white
person. What did that mean?

"I loved being married," said Irene, lowering her gaze
to her glass. "I was finally calm enough to look about me
without panic." She shrugged. For years of her marriage
there had been so little panic she'd fallen asleep. So that
if you asked her what she did between 1965 and 1968,
she would probably recall only that those three years
amounted to one day, really, and that on that day one of
her neighbors had invited her to go fishing, and she had
declined.

"That's *it*," said Anastasia, "sort of. When you're not
living with someone it's like all sides of you are exposed at
once. Right? But when you are living with someone at
least one side of you is covered. Panic can still strike, but
not on that one side." She wanted to emphasize how this
was especially true in the case of race. That, having put
race aside as a cause of concern, she could now concentrate
on whatever assaults were in store for the other facets of

herself. But of course Irene would say she had not put aside race, only chosen a different side of it to live on. Blacks who had not had her experience were rarely inclined to appreciate her point of view; though she understood this, she still thought it spoke of limitation on their part.

"What happened to Source, Peace and Calm, Bliss and Co.—South America? Do you have the baby here with you?" Irene asked, looking about the bar as if she expected to see Bliss crawling under the tables in their direction.

Anastasia looked glum. Her cheeks, Irene noticed, sagged when she wasn't smiling. But this was no worse than what the years had done to Irene's own face.

Anastasia had switched to Mai Tais; in her mind, Alaska and Hawaii were very close—they were so distant from the other forty-eight states. She said, sullenly, taking a sip from her small, overdressed drink (in addition to the traditional umbrella, there were tiny snowshoes), "I have a permanent tremor under my eye now—you know that? I've had it since living in San Francisco. It comes and goes. Now that I've mentioned it, watch for it. It is sure to make its appearance before long."

Her right eye, underneath the eye, really, began to quiver.

"I *hate* that," she said, clapping her palm over it. "I don't know *where* they are. They may have gone to South America, for all I know. I don't know *what* happened to Bliss." She giggled.

"*Some*thing happened to bliss," said Irene, and giggled also. The two of them whooped, thumped their glasses on the table and rumbled their feet underneath. A solicitous waitress inquired if there were something she could do.

"Find out what happened to bliss!" they said, laughing up at her and ordering doubles.

"After a couple of years I began to fall apart again," said Anastasia. "Facial tic, constant colds, diarrhea, you name it. You should have seen me. My hair looked like brass *wire*, my skin had more eruptions than Indo*nesia*. My *teeth* were loosening. . . . If I was so tranquil, why was this happening? I hadn't slept a whole night since I couldn't remember when, either.

"But I didn't want to leave Source, oh no! Listen, *average* sex, but with great dope, a little music, somebody above you to intercede with God, and the world outside your im*mediate* premises fails to interest."

"*Hum*mmmm," said Irene.

"Leave Source? Not on your life! Or *my* life, as the case was. Enter my parents—as screwed up as I was myself, but a mite put out that I was in the habit of talking to myself as easily as to strangers on the street." She shrugged. "Back to Arkansas. A few months of house arrest, no dope, church music (listen, the only reason Jehovah's Witnesses can sing is they've ripped off so many Baptists) and the realization that neither black nor white had ever known what to do with us in Arkansas. That we were freaks. And that it was my parents' ambivalence, as much as anything, that had driven us all nuts. They were horrified if my friends were poor and black, disappointed in my taste if they were black and middle class, and embittered if they were white; where was my racial pride?

"I married the first man who signed up from Arkansas to work on the Alaska pipeline. Found a job. Divorced him. *Voilà*."

Irene thought of Fania, whose interest in reading had finally been sustained by the slave narratives of black women so similar, she felt, to herself, and who would have read with keen interest the story Anastasia was now telling.

Was your mother white?

Yes, she pretty white; not white enough for white people. She have long hair, but it was kinda wavy. . . .

Were your children mulattoes?

No, Sir! They were all white. They looked just like him

159

... then he told me he was goin' to die ... and he said that if I would promise him that I would go to New York, he would leave me and the children free. ... He told me no person would know it (that I was colored) if I didn't tell it.*

"Did I ever tell you about Fania Evans?" asked Irene. "No? She was one of the women I tried to teach to read the newspaper. I had trouble because she refused to learn to read anything that hurt her. The world being what it is, this left very little news."

"Oh yes, I think I remember something about her," said Anastasia, in the spirit of the conversation. She didn't remember a word. "But wait a minute," she said, "let me really bring you up to date. The man I live with now is an Indian, an Aleut. Did I tell you that?"

"You probably tried to," said Irene, "but no saga of sexual superiority, womanlike tenderness or rippling muscles, *please.*"

"He does have it all," said Anastasia, happily, "but I won't mention it."

"Thanks," said Irene.

"We live in a small fishing village where the only industry is smoking salmon. That's all the women there know how to do. But as a white woman—" she grinned across the table at Irene, who at that moment was feeling unpleasantly sour, "or should I say as a non-Native? Anyway, they didn't expect me to know how to smoke salmon. When I did it along with them, they were delighted. It was as if I'd evolved. They don't know this yet, but I'm

* Rev. H. Mattison, *Louisa Picquet, the Octoroon: A Tale of Southern Slave Life* (New York, 1861), as quoted in *Black Women in Nineteenth-Century American Life,* edited, with an Introduction, by Bert James Lowenberg and Ruth Bogin (The Pennsylvania State University Press, University Park, Pa., and London, 1976).

on my way to being them." She paused. "I think really that Source was a fascist. Only a fascist would say nobody's anything. Everybody's *something*. Some*body*. And I couldn't feel like somebody without a color. I don't think anyone in America *can*. . . . Which really *is* pathetic. However, looking as I look, black wasn't special enough. It required two hours of explanation to every two seconds of joy." She paused again. "And it *was* two seconds."

"Gotcha," said Irene. She was so drunk by now that she understood everything Anastasia said as if she'd thought it herself. But she also forgot it at once.

"Now, tell me about Fania *Who*sis? I want to know all about her," said Anastasia.

"No," said Irene, "I'm too drunk."

"I'll order coffee," said Anastasia. "I also have to go to the toilet."

"So do I," said Irene, feeling her stomach muscles rebel against her control-top panty hose.

When they returned, a pitcher of coffee shaped like a moose's head awaited them. Irene was still mopping her face and neck with a wet paper towel, and Anastasia was taking a small container of honey from her handbag. She did not eat sugar.

For ten minutes they drank the strong coffee in silence. Eventually, their heads began to clear.

For the first time, Irene was aware of the people in the booth directly behind them. *Fifteen years ago,* a man's voice said, *they weren't allowed in places like this. No dogs, Eskimos or Indians Allowed. That's terrible,* a woman's voice replied. *Especially since it was their country,* a young man spoke, sneeringly. *But we developed it,* said the young woman, in sisterly explanation. *Oh, sure,* said the young man. *How can a woman say something so stupid? You've been developed yourself, only you're so dumb you think you like it.* The older woman's voice, attempting to keep the peace, spoke up, changing the subject. *Is it really all that much bigger than Texas? Oh, way bigger*, said the older man with pride.

All Irene had known about Alaska she'd read in an Edna Ferber novel. Now she had learned about gigantic turnips, colossal watermelons, marijuana that was not only legally grown, harvested and used, but that regularly grew twenty feet tall in the hot, intensely productive summers. She had learned that parkas were way beyond her budget and that mukluks made her feet sweat. The Eskimos and Indians she saw on the street looked like any oriental San Franciscan. Now her mind stuck on *fifteen years ago*, and her own witnessing of similar signs coming down in the South. But the signs had already done their work. For as long as she lived she knew she would be intimidated by fancy restaurants, hotels, even libraries, from which she had been excluded before.

"It's nice to look at you. To tell you I *enjoy* the way you look." Anastasia reached over and caressed Irene's cheek. Then she got up, bent over Irene, and very deliberately gave her a kiss, pressing her lips firmly against the warm, jasmine-smelling brown skin. "I always envied you, before," she said.

"It's supposed to be the other way around," said Irene, smiling.

"It was so *miserable*, growing up, not resembling any of my friends. Resembling, instead, the people they hated! And oh, black people were so con*fused*. They showed me in every way they envied me because my color and my hair made things 'easy' for me, but those other people, with hair and skin like mine, they despised, and took every opportunity to tell me so. And another thing, I'm really rather homely, even funny-looking. But I was convinced very early that I was a beauty. I was never permitted an accurate reflection of myself."

162

"Why do I think you must have enjoyed it, at least a little?" asked Irene.

"Of course I was glad to be the 'princess' for a long time," said Anastasia. "I don't deny it. But never without *such* feelings of guilt. Why was I picked to be Snow White, Cinderella, and any other white lady in distress, when *all* my classmates were better actresses? Why did the boys *flock* to me, in high school, when I couldn't dance, was afraid to make jokes, and had a mother who let them know the darker shades of black were not acceptable? Oh, finally I got so *tired* of black people, that was why I decided to go to college in the North. They finally seemed to me—merely thoughtless, and selfish, and so fucked up over color it was embarrassing. Then in the sixties they started crying 'freedom!' but certainly this wasn't for the likes of me."

"You already had your freedom," said Irene. "The freedom to go either way."

"To be *thrown* either way, you mean," said Anastasia. "Even you got in on the throwing."

Like most people who have come to believe they are better than they are, Irene resented the notion that she could be intolerant. She sat up very straight to listen to this.

"Remember Styron's *Nat Turner?*" asked Anastasia.

"Vaguely," said Irene, who had worked diligently over a decade to erase the book from memory.

"Well, I remember it very well. One of our professors had the nerve to teach it to our class, and when you couldn't make him see what an insult Styron's *monster* was to the memory of the real Nat Turner, you were so mad you wouldn't speak to anyone on campus for days. That was when you started to drink a lot. And you were this shining example of sober, intelligent black people-hood, too!" Anastasia laughed. "Not only drunk every evening, but *nastily* drunk. Throwing *up*, starting *fights*,

---

calling people *names*. And they couldn't really *expel* you; you were the only really *dark* black student they had. And they *adored* you. But you said that was shit because they could *not* adore you and teach Styron's version of your history at the same time. Which made absolute sense to me."

"Hypocrites, the whole bunch," said Irene.

"And so were you. You *loved* being adored. Being exceptional. Representing the race. I knew, from the backhanded way *I* was treated, that they were hypocrites. I mean, they knew *I* was black, I just didn't *look* black. I never got any of the attention you got, and I could have used some, because those white folks were just as strange to me as they were to you. But you thought everything was *fine* until the hypocrisy touched you."

"Oh, if only we didn't have to live with what we have been," thought Irene, feeling a surge of self-disgust. What Anastasia said was basically true; but even worse was the realization that she had viewed Anastasia in the same "backhanded" way her professors had. In fact, *she* had never been able to consider her entirely black, and in subtle ways had indicated a lack of recognition, of trust.

"We had gone for a walk, to help clear your head," Anastasia was saying. "I understood what you were feeling because, wonder of wonders, *I* felt the same way. I followed you back to your room—do you realize you were the only student in the whole school who *had* a private room? Remember what you said to me?"

She hadn't *wanted* the private room, was all she could think, but that was not the answer to the question. Irene thought and thought. She couldn't remember. She had been assigned the private room because she was "different," *that* she could remember.

"As we were going into your room, I said, 'God, I know *just* how you feel.' And you turned, right there in the doorway, and you blocked me from coming into your room, and as you closed the door very slowly in my face, you said, very distinctly, and as if you'd thought about it for a long time, 'How could you possibly?' "

Irene felt as if live coals had been thrown down her back.

"Wait, wait a minute," she said with relief, having found a straw to clutch. "Styron's book wasn't even out then. That was two or three years later!"

Anastasia looked at her, and pushed her palms against the edge of the table in front of her.

"So?" she said. "It was the same book with a different name. There's at least *one* racist best seller published a year."

Irene groaned. "I was *drunk*."

"Not good enough," said Anastasia.

"No."

Anastasia was glad she was finally able to say these things. All her life she had felt compelled to take and take and take from black people, anything they gave. Compliments and curses with the same benign, understanding silence. After all, she was exempt from their more predictable suffering, and must not presume to assert herself. Now that was over, and it felt good.

She realized that something was shifting, in her talk with Irene. They were still linked together, but it was not, now, the link of race, which had been tenuous in any case, and had not held up. They were simply two women, choosing to live as they liked in the world. She wondered if Irene felt this.

"You were my objective correlative," said Irene. She struggled over each word, as if she would unmask her own confusion in this matter, or else. "You see, my great fear in college was that I could hardly avoid becoming an ordinary bourgeois success. I was bright, energetic, attractive, with never a *thought* of failure, no matter *what* sociologists say. Those students who were destined, within ten years, to know the names of the designers of their shoes and luggage, to vacation in Europe once a year and read two best sellers every five—while doing a piss-poor job of teaching our children—scared the hell out of me. That life, and not the proverbial 'getting pregnant and dropping out of school,' represented 'the fate worse than death.'

"Your dilemma was obvious. You, even *objectively* speaking, didn't know who you were. What you were going to do next; which 'you' would be the one to survive. At the same time that I condemned you for your lack of commitment to anything I considered *useful*, I used you as the objectification of my own internal dilemma. In the weirdest way, your confusion made mine seem minor by comparison. For example, I understood that the episode with Source was a short cut, for you, to the kind of harmonious, multiracial community that you could be happy in, and which I also believed possible to create in America. But politically this is a shaky vision. It was, in a way, *convenient* for me to think how *much more* shaky your 'dope & guru' program was. I was looking toward 'government' for help; you were looking to Source. In both cases, it was the wrong direction—*any* direction that is away from ourselves is the wrong direction."

"Ah, ah," said Anastasia, shaking her head from side to side, though the "ah, ah" was affirmative. "I was attracted to you because your destiny seemed so stable. Whatever else, you would remain a black woman. Black women, even the bourgeois successes, don't desert."

"Can't desert. Some of them certainly would if they could."

Anastasia laughed, as did Irene.

Anastasia now felt smug. Whatever *she* was, she thought, her child, which she hoped to have someday, would be a

Native American, once more and at last at the beginning
of things.

"You know," she said thoughtfully, rising and collecting
her things, because although it was still disconcertingly
bright outside, it was after midnight, "Source made us
use his name as our mantra during meditation, so there'd
be no part of our consciousness he was excluded from.
But you know how mantras are: at first they sound like
someone's name and you keep getting that person in your
mind. But soon the name becomes just a sound. For me,
the sound became a longing and then a direction for my
life." She shrugged. "I knew I had to merge this self with
something really elemental and stable, or it would shatter
and fly away." She smiled, thinking of the man she loved.

"You're happy to be going home to him, eh?" said Irene.

"Positively *ecstatic*," said Anastasia, beaming.

"Write," said Irene. "I've missed you."

"You *have*?" asked Anastasia.

Irene hugged her with a hug that was not an embrace
of shoulders; she hugged her whole body, feeling knee
against knee, thigh against thigh, breast against breast,
neck nestled against neck. She listened to their hearts
beating, strong and full of blood.

As they left the bar they passed a group of tourists who
were pointing off merrily into the distance. Irene and
Anastasia looked in the direction they were pointing and
began to smile. They thought they were finally seeing the
great elusive mountain, a hundred miles away. They were
not. It was yet another, nearer, mountain's very large feet,
its massive ankles wreathed in clouds, that they took such
pleasure in.